THE FIRST
ECHO

Illustrations by K.N.Pantarotto
Cover Design by K.N.Pantarotto
Map Design by K.N.Pantarotto
Typseset by Crystal Peake Type
ECHO font by Imagex Fonts
Rights administered by D.H. at Imagex fonts. All rights reserved. Used by permission.
Odinson font by Iconian Fonts
Rights administered by D.Z. at Iconian fonts. All rights reserved. Used by permission.
Map Cartography brushes by StarRaven on Deviantart.

ISBN: 978-1-9992389-0-2

First Edition

THE FIRST ECHO

K.N. PANTAROTTO

Thank you to all the wonderful people in my life
that never doubted me when that is all I ever did.

IIVONA

No worse
DANGER IS MORE
FRIGHTENING THAN
A FORCE OF NATURE.

PROLOGUE

Hard breaths and heavy footsteps broke the silence of peaceful dusk as a lithe, young redhead ran through the dense trees as though the wind was chasing her. The orange light of the setting sun illuminated her back against the ever-growing darkness of the forest. The long, black cloak draped over her shoulders and fluttered wildly behind her, but because of its thin material, it made little noise as she ran through the woods. In fact, it made just enough noise for her brother to hear her running. He needed to know where she was. Their plan sounded simple enough when spoken out loud, but actually going through with it would be difficult. The girl ran like prey from a predator, but she was the only predator right then.

Her prey was the king of the forest—the Hirzla.

These creatures were so highly evasive that, when

sighted it seemed like an illusion. They looked like stags, but they moved like ghosts. Sightings were rare and captures were impossible. Their ability to escape was legendary in her kingdom. In her experience, no one had ever caught one. Today was the day. She could feel it in her heart. There was nothing in the world she needed more than to trap this stag. This choice was not an impulse. It was a carefully calculated journey. If they succeeded today, it would be the first choice of many to accomplish their real goal. She didn't want the stag dead like the rest of her people who thought the creatures of this forest were cursed. She just needed to break one of its bones.

It was certain.

It was written in the stars.

Crack.

There it was.

She came to an abrupt stop.

It had stepped on the small trap of branches she had laid down before beginning this chase. The creature had come to its usual stop. She knew it was close enough to hit with a dart because she had followed it on this same path, on the same day for five years in a row. Every time they went through this chase, they would fail miserably. The last time she had tripped over a tree branch and couldn't walk for several weeks. That had never stopped her or hindered her progress. She was a quick learner. Even though she'd only spotted the stag twice in five years, she knew that was more than anyone else in the world could say.

"Now!" A man's voice shouted through the trees. The word resounded in her mind like an alarm. The redhead looked wildly around to focus on the direction of his voice. It had jumped to a different place from where she had last seen the creature. By some miracle her brother had wrapped his arms around the stag's neck. He'd never done so before. He'd only ever got behind it. That was the redhead's cue to shoot the dart. She would only get half a second to do so. The last four times she had, her brother had been the one to fall to the ground unconscious.

With a short prayer and a quick shot, the dart hit the stag, and it stumbled over its own feet in a dance of confusion. The man let out a short, maniacal laugh that was muffled by the cloth mask he was wearing. The creature hit the dirt with a giant thud. Its big, black eyes fluttered closed.

There was a moment when the siblings couldn't believe they had actually done it. They both stared in silence at the stag in front of them. It was much larger than the common elk. Its antlers were enormous. An unearthly green glow surrounded the creature as if its fur had been lit on fire; a fire that could not be put out. Even when it was knocked out like this, the glow around its body was still moving. When the wind picked up around them, so did the green flames.

"I can't believe you didn't screw that up," said the redhead as she knelt next to the animal, waving a hand in front of its eyes to make sure it was unconscious. While she regained her breath, she took a moment to wave her hand through the illusion of flames that surrounded its body. They were warm like a beautiful summer's day. It was the kind of warmth you felt from sitting comfortably in the sun, but not feeling hot enough to sweat. The unnerving heat gave her goosebumps.

"Stop playing. Work quickly. That was a heavy dose of sleeping rash root. I'm glad you didn't hit me this time, but we don't know how much time we have before it wakes," demanded the man who was fully cloaked from head to toe. It seemed he had snapped out of his daze much quicker than his sister. Still caught in wonderment, the woman handed him a hammer made of steel and a chisel from a shoulder pack that she kept under her cloak. He took a shaky breath in and gulped down. The girl readied an open vial underneath one of the stag's antlers, which she had around her neck on a string. When she was positioned and ready, she nodded to her brother. The two exchanged an unsettling look as the man's hands trembled.

"Well... we've gotten this far," he muttered before he lifted the hammer above his head and with all his strength, he brought it down on to the chisel placed at the base of the stag's antler.

CRACK.

The sound eerily echoed through the forest like a cursed symphony that should have never been played. The bone broke in two unclean pieces, and a strange green substance oozed out of the base of the antler. The girl caught as much as she could with the small glass vial as the animal slowly awoke in a daze. It grunted, and its eyes shot open. It began to jerk its head around wildly as it tried to get off its side to stand, making it difficult to catch anything in the vial. The girl's hands suffered the wrath of the stag as the green liquid smothered them. It began to burn her skin, and she clenched her teeth to fight the pain. The burning was unexpected. She hadn't known it could do that. No one had attempted this before, so the predators were learning as they hunted.

Suddenly, the stag got to its feet in the blink of an eye. Both siblings looked bewildered as they had only just seen it wiggling on the ground, and the next moment, it was on its feet just a couple of strides away from them. The creature stood and turned to look back at them as if it were offended and slightly drunk. The wild green glow that surrounded it was brighter than ever, but around its broken antler, a small black cloud had formed.

With one last grunt, the creature disappeared from existence in front of their eyes.

The girl seethed, suddenly remembering the pain of her burnt hands. Her brother took the vial from her and closed it as she carefully tried to clean them.

"Next time, you hold the vial." The redhead sulked at the marks she'd been left with. "And don't forget to grab the antler," the girl added. The man scoffed and shook his head at her. There wouldn't be a next time. After this go, the gods would surely be angered.

Her brother reached for the antler on the ground, not thinking much of the action. When he came within an inch of the antler, it erupted and a nasty green flame bit the palm of his hand. The man cursed, and his reflexes kicked the thing away. As he did so, his sister gasped and jumped up.

"What if we need more?" she shrieked.

"We have plenty for now, calm down," he retorted and shook the pain from his hand as much as he could. Nervously, her eyes darted around the forest. It was almost completely dark now. The little bit of light that the sky emitted couldn't get through the dense trees.

"You don't think we killed it, do you? What if someone else finds the body?"

"Well, hopefully the thing burns them too!" Rolling his eyes the man walked off into the forest without warning, visibly annoyed with his sister's questions. "And it's not people you have to worry about. If we accidentally killed the thing, we're going to have to keep looking over our shoulder for death himself."

I
THE FIND

The warm glow of the afternoon sun seeped through the leaves of the lush forest illuminating a stag eating peacefully in a clearing. Atop a tall tree just outside of the clearing sat a young girl with big, brown doe eyes homed in on the unsuspecting stag. In perfect silence she unsheathed a small throwing knife strapped to her calf, careful not to lose her balance as she did so, and pulled her throwing arm back behind her head.

"Kaapo!"

Startled, Echo's hand slipped on the branch she was gripping but she caught herself from falling just in time. Within the next second she straightened herself and looked down at her body to reassess her positioning on the tree. Shifting, she maintained her balance carefully, making sure not to fall to the ground from twenty some feet high. Once she was comfortable again, she squinted into the clearing of the forest. *Good* she thought, her prey was still in sight. But now her imbecile of a brother was up to his old tricks.

"Kaapo, you fool, go back! I already told you, this one is mine!" She snapped at him at a volume much too loud to be called a whisper but not loud enough for her brother to hear.

Echo's older brother by two years, Kaapo, had been on her tail since the two had entered the thick forest. The young man had chased down what she had tracked down very skilfully. What she attacked strategically, he attacked with a storm, and now he stood at the edge of the clearing where her prey sat in the middle. Even though she had told him exactly eighteen times before she left in the morning to leave her alone and let her hunt by herself for a change.

It was difficult for her brother to obey such a request. The young man had such an easy way of hunting. Kaapo was the family favourite for three reasons: he was the first-born child, he was a boy, and he was *special*. Kaapo didn't only have a way with animals. He had a way of turning into them, which was how he was getting the stag in the middle of the clearing to stay put, even after Kaapo had made such a ruckus when he came into the clearing in disguise.

Kaapo stood at the edge of the clearing now, his body mimicking that of the stag's, which seemed to confuse, but keep the attention of, the real creature.

When the stag tapped its hoof, Kaapo tapped back gingerly to hold its interest. Its ears went up and it grunted at Kaapo. He seemed to notice something different about this creature. Animals are smart…too smart. They can smell and hear things differently, looks alone aren't enough to convince them. This stag looked as if he was coming to the conclusion that this creature was not his brother, but instead—a bloodhound.

Before letting the animal think anymore about his illusion, Kaapo lunged forward at the stag. As he sailed through the air, the young man's body took its original form of a five-foot-eleven-inch man with a muscular build and darkly tanned skin wearing nothing but shorts. It didn't take him long to crack the stag's neck.

Even though the stag had died, its rage filled Echo. She, very skilfully, manoeuvred her way down the tree, missing a few branches as she did so. Landing with an earthly thud, Echo moved toward her brother and pushed him off the dead creature. As he fell backwards into a tumble he began to laugh at her temper. Seething, she picked little leaves and branches out of her chestnut-brown hair that ended just past her shoulders.

"And what did you plan to kill it with from the tree? You're no good with a bow!" The young man asked smugly as he lay on the ground.

"My knife!" She yelled, frustrated with his calm manner.

"You're no good with that either!" The young man laughed and then sat upright. It looked as if he was about to explain something, when he yelped out in pain instead. The change in his behaviour made Echo think that he was fooling around.

"I had it! Why must you do that?" She barked and kicked at the dirt in front of Kaapo as he winced in pain and held his back. "Oh, what now?" Echo asked in a disbelieving tone. When he examined the hand that he had held to his side he noticed it was red with his own blood and jumped up at the sight of it. Echo seemed just as startled. "Is that yours or the stag's?" she shrieked.

In a stunned daze Kaapo shook his head unsure of how to answer. Echo pulled Kaapo towards her and examined his back. She noticed a gash slowly oozing blood down his hip. Bewildered, she looked around the forest floor to see what could have done it.

As she rummaged through the piles of leaves and sticks she came across a stag's antler. For a moment, she wondered if it belonged to the stag her brother had just tackled, but she quickly noticed it still had both of its antlers.

Crouching on the forest floor, Echo inspected the object further and realized that it was no ordinary antler. It was about the size of her forearm and it was much thicker and curvier than any other antler she had seen before. It could have been a trick of the eye, but Echo thought she saw a faint green, glowing light emanating from it. Without further hesitation she bagged the antler in a satchel she wore close to her body, and looked at her brother.

"We need to get you to the healer. We'll leave the stag for now. I'll tell Hanuel to get it later." Echo wrapped her brother's arm around her shoulder as well as she could even though she was ten inches shorter than him. In fearful silence, they walked back to their village. Kaapo winced with every step.

When the two arrived at their settlement they immediately went to the healer's hut. Echo knocked on the door with urgency. The two waited in silence as they heard the woman hustle around on the other side of it. The woman quickly opened the door with her index finger to her lips and a demanding look on her face. The siblings stayed silent as they entered. The only thing to be heard were the low grunts of Kaapo and the midday chirping of birds in the distance.

Eira, the healer, was nearing sixty-five years of age. Even though she was the healthiest in the clan, she didn't show it. Her hair was a snowy white mop wound tightly in a braid with only a few silvery wisps escaping it. Her eyes were black with many wrinkles surrounding them, but the left one was plagued by cataracts and the middle of it was almost as white as her hair. She looked as if she could be the siblings' grandmother, but she was not. In her earlier days as a healer, her abilities were the strongest in the clan. With one touch she could heal a wound, but she noticed after years of doing it, it would age her more quickly than others. After that discovery, she spent her life researching which herbs and plants would heal her tribe in the sacred forest, in fear of killing herself too quickly.

THE FIRST ECHO

The older woman pointed to the bed that she wanted Kaapo to sit on which was furthest from the door. Eira then grabbed a bowl off of her working table, walked right over to Kaapo and had her hands on his back in seconds, wiping away the blood with a rag soaked in astringent. Kaapo winced with pain as he grasped Echo's hand for support.

"My dear, what on earth did you anger?" Eira asked.

"Me, mostly," Echo said in an agitated tone.

"Echo, you barely have the heart to hunt an animal. I don't believe for a second you did this."

"It was a joke. I didn't do it to him but he wouldn't let me hunt alone, and when he killed my hunt this goon rolled over on a very sharp antler on the forest floor!" Kaapo huffed and rolled his eyes.

"Lower your voice, Echo." Eira shot the girl a demanding look.

"As if you were going to kill it..." The young man mumbled under his breath.

"Kaapo you need to let her learn. Life cannot continue without death. It is a cycle we must contribute to; we kill the animals we need, they give us the life we need. Nothing more and nothing less." While Eira explained the circle of life Echo pulled out the antler from the pack over her shoulder and inspected it further. The glowing had stopped. Consumed with fixing her brother's gash and teaching a life lesson, Eira didn't notice what Echo was holding, but when she looked over she did a double take.

"Echo, *that* was the antler he rolled onto in the

forest?"

"Yes… and if I'm being honest, when I first picked it up it looked gree—"

"It was." Eira cut her off. With a swift movement she took Kaapo's hand and made him hold the rag to his side. The quick movement made him wince again. With the urgency of a mother goose guarding her nest Eira grabbed the antler out of Echo's hands and rushed over to a table on the other side of the cabin. She lay the antler down on it and rummaged through a basket of things just to the left of where she placed it. Even though the basket was filled with all kinds of primitive-looking tools she knew exactly where the small metal hammer lay. With one swift hit she cracked the antler open at the base and her strange eyes focused in on the fluorescent green sap oozing from the broken bone. The siblings didn't look much alike, in terms of their facial features, but they now shared the same confused look as they watched the healer in her flurry.

"What in Providence is that?" Kaapo asked before wincing as he moved the rag a little higher up his gash.

"I've only ever seen the bones, and I had a suspicion… I believe it's a Hirzla antler. Did you find the body of it?" Eira asked dazed, yet quizzically, still staring at the fluorescent green ooze. The old woman grabbed a small, wooden spoon and scooped some of it up before it disappeared through the slats in the wooden table. Echo watched as the healer put what little green ooze she collected into a small glass vial of which she didn't have many. Echo shook her head in response.

"No, the only body on the forest floor was this goon's," Echo raised her hand to point at her brother, "and the stag I tracked into the clearing. That one had both its antlers when Kaapo so *gracefully* killed it." Echo rolled her eyes as she was still taking jabs at her brother whenever she could.

"I want you to take this piece and create a weapon from it. This is yours now and yours only. Kaapo may have been wounded by it but you found it. You know how sacred this animal is don't you?" asked Eira as she held out the base of the antler to the girl. Echo took it hesitantly.

"If I remember correctly the Hirzla appearing to you is some kind of ancestor connecting to you?" Echo shrugged, she never did pay much attention to her lessons. She tried, but her memory was terrible. As she focused on the jagged top of the antler, she took it from Eira's hands.

"For our people, finding the bones are a warning. You must make a weapon with whatever you find to protect yourself from what is to come. There were only two others in our history to come across a hoof turned into a club and a leg turned into a spear," explained Eira as she travelled back to Kaapo to bandage his body. "When the Hirzla appears to you, it is an ancestor warning you that your next choice could have dire consequences such as Draviden when the Hirzla stopped him and led him to his people...there." Eira patted Kaapo's bandage lightly and looked him sternly in the eyes. "No shifting until that wound scabs over. The last time you did that you almost bled to death." Kaapo sighed and looked down at the ragged bandage around his waist.

"Well, that's no fun."

The old woman smirked and shooed him out of her home. When Echo went to follow behind him, Eira stepped in between the girl and the door. Even though she was shorter than Echo with a slight hunch in her back, it didn't make her any less intimidating. Eira was the tough love type. Even if she was giving you life-saving advice, the way she delivered it was nothing less than blunt.

"You hum like your mother did when her powers came in. You need to relax Echo. The more strain you put on yourself, the longer it will take to develop." Echo's facial expression never matched her inner thoughts. She was suddenly flustered and unsure of what to say after Eira's words. Her face stayed completely still and she tried not to roll her eyes at the healer as she already doubted her.

"As if I'm even going to devel—"

"Your mother took a long time to bloom as well, and now look at her; she makes the world bloom around her. Your brother shifted at this age, and he hasn't stopped since!" Eira touched the middle of Echo's forehead with her wrinkled finger, and with each word that she said next she tapped her forehead gently, "Relax child. It will come."

Echo gulped down and Eira moved out of her way. Walking away from the cabin slowly, Echo could suddenly feel her heart racing with the pressure of wanting to possess any kind of extraordinary power like the rest of her family. Every day she wished she'd develop something, and when she turned sixteen she figured that she might have to give up on the dream. The more she thought about it, she didn't know how she couldn't have developed something within her life by this age. What with her father and his incredible strength, and her mother with her ability to control any flora around her. Then there was Kaapo, the boy who saved his tribe by turning into a bear. A mountain bear to be more specific - the strongest creature in the sacred forest, and it didn't end there. Ever since he shifted into a bear he didn't stop. He could shift into any animal he saw. He was a prodigy in their clan.

Ringwaldr; their father's second-hand man with the gift of foresight, told Kaapo what to do when the opportunity arose after he had a vision. Echo wished with all her might that Ringwaldr would come to her with a similar vision. She just wanted to change. To be someone better in everyone's eyes.

I'm useless, she thought to herself as she kicked the dirt in front of her.

"Eh, watch where you're kicking that would you!" Hanuel, Echo's childhood friend smirked up at her. Startled, her eyes widened, and then when she saw him she eased into a more comfortable expression. "Did I catch you in a thought?" The young man asked, his smirk slowly fading. He watched her intently with deep, black eyes peeking from under a curly mess of dark golden brown hair. His hair also covered his large ears that could hear a pin drop from miles away. "What's wrong Echo?" he asked. She shook her head and sighed.

"Kaapo hurt himself but he'll live, and what's wrong with me? Well, nothing more than usual," she said. Hanuel nodded in agreement. He knew all too well about her desire to be like the rest of her tribe. It was his duty as her oldest friend to listen to her go on a tangent as they scouted the forest.

Both Hanuel and Echo were scouts in training. For two years now they spent most of their days in the sacred forest or at their village's border watching for any threats. Hanuel with his talents of seeing in the dark and hearing extremely well made him born for the job. It was either be a soldier or be a scout for him. He chose the latter because his father, Rythyn, was the leader of the Hemera tribe's army, and as much as he loved his father, he didn't want to work with him. Echo didn't have an extraordinary power. All she was good at was climbing. She often wondered if she was only training as a scout because her father, Asmund, didn't know what else to do with her. Scouts were important to Hemera for their many skills, but they weren't required to have special abilities. Echo had learned that she wasn't delicate enough for making clothes. She couldn't stomach killing animals for cooking, even though she was trying her hardest to learn to hunt, and she never had the patience for agriculture. If her father weren't the leader and a bit overprotective, she would have tried her hand at combat. Although, she was sure she wasn't made for that either.

THE FIRST ECHO

Asmund, the leader of Hemera, made it quite obvious that he was concerned about Echo's lack of extraordinary abilities. These abilities were what their tribe, the Hemera tribe, was known for. Whenever he would see her, which wasn't very often in the day, he would constantly ask her if she had exhibited any kind of ability. Sometimes it got on her nerves so much that she'd very convincingly tell him yes, and start some outlandish story about her saving someone with her newfound ability but the stories always had a sardonic undertone. He never believed her when she did it because she would use the same flowery language and body movements her brother did when he was pulling a practical joke on someone. The one thing that Echo and Kaapo had in common was their terrible sense of humour and their father knew that all too well.

"So where were you off to friend?" Hanuel asked in a soft voice, hoping to take Echo's mind off things.

"I'm not quite sure actually." She looked up at the sky turning red with dusk and held up her hand over her eyes, wiping her forehead in an exasperated manner. "I was hoping to find some things in the forest before nightfall but it seems a little late now." Shrugging, the boy walked closer to Echo and nudged her shoulder. Without any sort of warning he took off running towards the forest.

"Bet I can beat you there!" he bellowed. Echo let out a startled laugh and took off after her friend through a few cabins and down a dirt path that led back into the trees.

2
THE PLAN

Tired and out of breath, Hanuel came to a stop only a few feet into the forest. The light of the sunset only reached so far into the brush. The rest of it was covered in a familiar darkness, one that the two friends could navigate through even in the dead of night. They would never dare to without reason but if the situation arose, it would be something they could map out with little effort. They'd spent so many days and nights at the forest's edge, watching for threats and talking through the night. They both knew it as well as they knew the back of their hands. Echo came into the brush after him, her breath just as heavy as Hanuel's.

"I think I win this time," Hanuel said after he'd caught his breath.

"I'll give you that. I've never been able to beat you running, but climbing, that's another story." Echo said smugly, and began to climb up the nearest tree with practised ease.

"You know I hate following you up there. What are you even looking for?" Hanuel groaned.

"Materials." Echo mindlessly answered back. She began to pull off dead-looking tendrils from the tree and stuff them into her shoulder pack.

"Well it's not getting any brighter down here. Is there something you need from the ground?" Hanuel asked with a sigh.

"Hmm, a sharp rock maybe?" Echo answered and Hanuel started digging his moccasin into the dirt and leaves on the forest floor. When his foot came across something hard he picked it up and tested its sharpness by feeling the edges of it with his thumb. When it didn't pass the test he threw it over his shoulder. It barely missed Echo as she came down the tree and let out a startled laugh. "My friend, first you almost push me over, now you're throwing rocks at me? Whatever did I do to you?" Echo asked him with a convincingly hurt expression on her face. Hanuel stood up and scratched the back of his head with a look of embarrassment. Hanuel looked back at the rock he'd just accidentally thrown her way and thought of a quick recovery.

"Oh, you didn't like that one? I was throwing it over at you to show you. We better keep looking then." Echo laughed and lightly shoved him as they both got back onto the forest floor to continue looking. Only a few minutes later Echo found one she was pleased with and the two began to leave the forest. Echo was placing the rock in the satchel over her shoulder when Hanuel lightly held her back by gently holding on to her forearm and turning her to look at him. He held a finger to his lips making sure she stayed quiet, and brought her attention over to some dead brush.

Her big, doe eyes followed a very small blue light glittering just above some dead brush half engulfed in darkness. There, danced a blue sprint. Blue sprints were a type of bird with airy wings and a blue glow. They looked like luminescent butterflies only with longer tails and the head of a hummingbird. The little creature danced in the air a bit and landed on the dead brush. Its wings slowly came to a halt as its light disappeared in the blink of an eye. It instantly started to curl up and die. Its death made the dead brush around the two young adults lush and vibrant again. It turned such a vibrant green in an instant, that now the brush glowed in the semi-lit forest. Seeing the transformation from start to end, Echo gasped as her eyes settled on the animal, its fragile little body lay lifeless on one of the branches.

"Poor thing, I always hate when that happens," Echo breathed and Hanuel turned to her with a small sympathetic grin.

"You're supposed to thank them, not feel sorry for them. Hasn't Eira taught you anything Echo?" Echo scrunched up her face like a two-year-old that didn't get her way.

"No, I'm fairly stubborn, haven't you realized?" Hanuel smirked, wrapped his arm around her shoulders and led her out of the forest.

"You know by now that things have to die in order for others to live, right? Always feeling bad for them is a sign of your empathy, yes, but the cycle of life is not something to pity, it is something to thank, it will only continue to hurt you if..."

"If you continue to let it," Echo chimed in a mocking tone. "I've heard Eira's speech many times, and to be honest, she's much more intimidating than you with her intense eyes and silver hair. You and that curly mess on your head with that smug grin are not very convincing Hanuel," Echo said calmly squishing both of his cheeks together with one of her hands as they walked back down the dirt path to the roaring campfire for dinner. Hanuel smirked and squished her cheeks in retaliation, which made them both laugh at each other. The sunset was a red line on the horizon, and now the giant bonfire surrounded by the tribe's people was more of a light source than the sky. The smell of ash and roasting pork filled Echo's nose and she smiled in relief.

"Food." Hanuel inhaled the pleasant smell and left Echo's side to cut in line at the spit. He jumped in front of another friend named Sturla, who was just a bit shorter than him, with longer waist-length, brown hair and the same black eyes. The young man gave Hanuel a small shove and laughed as he feigned impatience. Then Hanuel shrugged at him as if he didn't jump in front of a hungry person in line for food. Echo decided to look around for her brother and parents first, but she could see neither of them around the fire where a small crowd had formed. Thinking Kaapo might be back at his cabin, she began to walk there to see if Kaapo wanted her to bring him anything to eat.

Calmly, Echo walked up the dirt path to the scattered cabins. A fire bringer from her tribe jogged by, flashing a pleasant smile and nodding to her as he passed. When he stopped at each torch on either side of the path he would light it with a simple wave of his hand. This happened every evening; one fire bringer would light all the path's torches as darkness neared. As Echo arrived at her brother's cabin she noticed a small group of young children playing a game on the cabin porch across from Kaapo's cabin. When she walked up to her brother's porch one of the young boys called out.

"Echo, come play with us!"

"I'll beat you lot later. Make sure you go eat something," she answered back in a motherly tone before knocking on Kaapo's door. There was barely a second in between her knock and the door swinging open. Echo was taken aback just a little. Expecting to be met by her brother's frame, who was barely a foot taller than her, and instead being met by her husky father whose height went above the door he'd opened, was a bit startling.

"Oh, hello father," Asmund nodded and let her past him. She quickly took notice of her mother, Takoda, tending to Kaapo's wound as he sat in his bed. Asmund was a much larger version of Kaapo, and Takoda was a wiser looking Echo. The subtle crow's feet around Takoda's eyes and Echo taking after her father's eye colour were the only thing that set the two women apart. Takoda's eyes were the colour of new spring grass, whereas Echo's were a deep, woody brown. The difference between Kaapo and his father, apart from their very different stature, was that Asmund had a long beard and usually kept his long hair down, whereas Kaapo kept his braided and liked to shave his facial hair.

At first Echo didn't notice the other male in the room. When she went to take a seat at the table across from where her mother was tending to Kaapo, she noticed him there.

"Good evening Echo." Ringwaldr, her father's right-hand man was there. He was the one with the gift of foresight who came to their tribe only two years prior to the present year. When he first arrived at the camp he had come with a vision that he said led him to the Hemera tribe.

In the vision, he saw Kaapo saving a group of scouts and hunters from a giant mountain bear by shifting into a mountain bear himself and scaring the other one off. The vision became so famously correct when Kaapo lived it out as it was told. The night Ringwaldr came to the Hemera tribe, he had been travelling for days, lost in the woods. The entire tribe was enthralled by Ringwaldr's stories from the desert, when he first arrived. His life experiences captivated everyone; the tribe especially loved him after he had told the story of how he survived the desert with just a crudely carved spear and the skull of a bird.

Every inch of the man's body except for his face

was marked with ink. Ringwaldr told everyone that the tattoos were of different tribal signs from around the world. The man was muscular enough to hold out in a fight with Asmund if he were to ever get in one, but Asmund would more than likely win because of his amazing strength and extra two inches in height he held over Ringwaldr.

"We need to discuss some things. I've been having visions as of late," Ringwaldr began. Echo's breath got caught in her throat and her stomach turned. For a moment she wished hard that one of his visions involved her doing something extraordinary. "War is coming and with your brother wounded we must send a scouting group into the forest within two nights time, making sure that once we send a messenger they don't take it as a threat. You will be in charge of putting a group together..."

"Darling, I want you to choose four other scouts to take with you. You will have to stay posted even through the dead of night, for one day and night. You must take a runner and a fire bringer when you are posted. If there are any signs of an army coming toward our camp that fire bringer has to signal us, and that runner has to get back as soon as possible. If you are uncomfortable with this task, we will choose the other scouts ourselves." Takoda interrupted Ringwaldr. His deep blue eyes glared at Takoda in silent retaliation. The man's hair was shoulder length and a lighter brown than everyone else's in the tribe but his skin was a darker shade of tan. You could easily tell he wasn't of Hemera descent but only when you took a longer look at him.

"No, I'll choose them," Echo answered calmly and looked to her father. "But war? Why? Who could we have possibly angered? We don't go anywhere beyond our territory." Crossing her arms over her chest she got up from the chair at the table and settled for a seat in a chair next to Kaapo's bed. She peaked at Kaapo's wound that her mother was now in the middle of rebandaging after she had put some kind of plant on it to help with the pain Echo assumed.

"We think it has something to do with who we've angered in the past. The Iivona tribe knows of our abilities but they've never been very accepting. It's been a while since any of our fire bringers have desiccated their land, but when you burn down someone's home they tend to hold a grudge," Asmund explained in his gruff tone.

"Hm, I wonder why," Echo said under her breath and Takoda shot a look of disapproval her daughter's way. It wasn't the first time Echo had made a snide comment about someone with a special ability in their tribe. To Echo it only seemed fair, as she was treated differently for not having a special ability, while others only saw a fire bringer burning something to the ground as a simple mistake that should be easily forgiven.

"We need you to have a group ready after sunrise tomorrow, but you should be in the forest the next sunrise after. That should give our messenger enough time to give them the message, and then it's just about how they take it. Get as close to the boundary lines within two days and hold post for three. You remember what the wall looks like, yes Echo?" Her mother asked sternly, and Echo nodded in response.

"And if we're seen?"

"You won't be," Ringwaldr responded without hesitation.

"But if we are?"

"That vision isn't strong enough."

"But you've *seen* it?" Echo leaned in on her chair, her face stern with intent. Maybe she was just angry because Ringwaldr didn't have a vision about her, or maybe she was annoyed that her brother being harmed suddenly put this responsibility all on her. Whatever it was, she was agitated, and it was coming out in the wrong way. "With all due respect, I understand you are good at what you see Ringwaldr, but to my knowledge, there are a lot of possible outcomes to your visions and you only get some sort of 'feeling' as to which one is right. What if you're not right this time?" The man's blue eyes glared at Echo as the room fell completely silent. Echo slowly realized that her rebellious speech didn't always rub Ringwaldr the right way.

"It is in your best interest to not doubt what I see. I've saved this tribe from many grievances before and I will continue to do that, but everyone in this room must cooperate for me to do so." The man seethed. You could see in his face that he was trying to hold back from retaliating more. Kaapo, now wide-eyed, figured he should take some of the attention off of the two in order to restore some peace in the room.

THE FIRST ECHO

"You're too smart to get caught Echo, and if you take Hanuel you'll know who's coming from several miles away." Echo stood and crossed her arms over her chest before going to stand in front of the door. She sighed at Kaapo's reasoning and glanced back to her father.

"Fine. In the meantime, what are we doing to keep Iivona calm?"

"As I said, we are sending out a messenger after this conversation, letting them know we want no conflict, only a resolution. We plan to meet with them within a week. If everything goes as planned, you may even see us pass you in the forest. We're hoping to resolve this issue with words. We have a new trading language for a reason, and even if they don't want to use it I know their old tongue." Asmund answered seemingly unbothered. He easily believed Ringwaldr's every word. Echo wished she could have that kind of confidence in him too, but she didn't like the idea of scouting the foreign territory.

"That reminds me, I should go send the messenger now." Takoda sighed and stood up from the end of Kaapo's bed, tiredly running a hand through her shoulder length brown hair. Ringwaldr stood from his chair at the same time.

"Don't worry Takoda. I'll handle the messenger myself." Ringwaldr then nodded to Asmund and brushed past Echo before leaving the cabin in an uncomfortable silence. Rubbing his forehead, Asmund sighed deeply before looking to his son.

"Have either of you eaten anything today?" he asked.

His husky tone sounded less intimidating and more nurturing when he spoke to his children about matters that didn't involve politics.

"No, I'll grab something and bring it to Kaapo."

"Thank you, darling. Kaapo, I'll be the first one at your side in the morning to check that bandage." Takoda flashed Kaapo a weak smile, and Asmund led her out of the cabin. The siblings shared a quick look before Echo nodded to Kaapo and stood up from the chair she was sitting in.

"I'll be back with some food."

"Yeah, if Hanuel didn't eat it all," Kaapo smirked and Echo rolled her eyes at his joke. She wasn't in the mood for banter. Her world felt like it was being held together by a frayed string that she was now in charge of holding on to and told not to drop. It seemed like everything could suddenly come crashing down and she would be to blame. Anytime her parents gave her a task she felt twice as obliged as Kaapo to have it completed. Being the runt of the family with no Hemera ability, she found herself feeling as if she had to jump over ten more hurdles than anyone else. She left the cabin and looked at the porch across from Kaapo's porch. It was completely dark and the children had left. Looking down the dirt path in the direction of the roaring bonfire she saw a figure she knew all too well.

"I saw you leave without getting food and I was just a little concerned that you wouldn't get any before I decided to finish it all." Hanuel grinned while holding up two ropes with big slabs of cooked boar tied to the end of them.

"You know you could just control yourself and not eat everything before I get to it." Echo replied.

"If I stopped eating the amount I do how would I ever keep up this handsome physique," he asked with an incredulous look. Echo shook her head at him and took the ropes from his hand.

"Come on, let's go feed and water my brother before he starts to grow more weeds out of that dense brain of his." The two went back into the cabin and set the meat on the table. Hanuel walked over to Kaapo and pulled a chair up to his bed.

"I heard she beat you in a fight again. What did she hit you with this time, friend? A stick? A rock?" Hanuel asked him in a fairly serious tone, and Kaapo joined in on the theatrics.

"She stabbed me well and good. Twisted the knife even. If I hadn't the strength of twelve men I would have died!" He winced dramatically and Echo shook her head with a sigh at their antics. She had been splitting up the pieces of meat to put on a plate for Kaapo as he and Hanuel made their jokes.

"Here!" She walked over and gently threw the plate down at the foot of his bed. "This is your own doing. You never would've gotten hurt if you had just listened to me."

"You know, you sound exactly like mom when you nag," Kaapo said as he took the plate from the edge of his bed and started in on his dinner. Echo was not at all amused by the comment and Hanuel snorted when he saw the look Echo was shooting at Kaapo as he mindlessly ate his food.

"You are absolutely clueless, and now that you've hurt yourself I'm left in charge when it should be you," she complained. Hanuel looked confusedly over at her.

"In charge of what?"

"Oh right, we have to go on a scout the day after tomorrow at sunrise, to watch the Iivona border for any signs of an army. Apparently we've angered them, and they're threatening us with war." Hanuel blinked a few times trying to take in all the information then furrowed his brow.

"That seems out of the ordinary. They usually keep to themselves," Hanuel said slowly as he scratched the back of his head.

"That's what I thought, but Ringwaldr has had a vision and my father takes Ringwaldr's visions very seriously. So, I was put in charge because the next heir in line has injured himself on a sharp thing."

While cleaning her hands on a nearby rag, Echo put her plate down on the table behind her as she finished chewing what remained in her mouth and pulled the antler out from her pack. Very abruptly she threw it over to Hanuel and he caught it in a cradle as if it were a newborn baby.

"A stag?"

"Oh no!" Echo let out, smacking herself in the forehead. "We left our catch in the forest. I never told Hanuel!" Kaapo grunted and shook his head in detest.

"I told mom before I came into my cabin. She

already sent out Manson to collect the stag, its fine." Kaapo answered with a mouth full of food.

"So you fought a stag and got hit in the side?" Turning to Kaapo with a confused look, Hanuel asked as he was still trying to piece together the actual story.

"No, no, no. He killed my hunt, and then rolled over on a Hirzla antler on the ground and hurt himself. He's not getting any credit for anything. The boy can get into a fight with a bear but he can't protect himself from sharp things on the forest floor." Echo rolled her eyes and Kaapo handed Echo his plate with a smirk while she was visibly irritated by his blithe behaviour. She tore it from his hand and threw it on the table with the other dirty metal plate as Hanuel took to squinting at the bone as if he were waiting for it to give its side of the story.

"Wait, this is a Hirzla antler? You know what that means don't you?"

"Why does everyone keep saying that?" Echo said in exasperation and took a seat set next to the table. Seeing that he may have upset her Hanuel sighed and handed her back the antler.

"It's just that everything I've ever heard about Hirzla is that, if you're lucky enough to see one, they're a warning." A chill crept up Echo's spine now and she was very quickly piecing things together in her mind. Very awful things were fuelled by paranoia.

"Great, so I've got an ominous warning the day before I'm put in charge of a scouting that's *supposedly* going to go well?"

"It seems that way." Kaapo shrugged and Echo was continuously getting frustrated with his lack of concern. Kaapo let out a small laugh when he noticed how disarrayed Echo was becoming.

"Echo, calm down. There's a certain amount of old folklore our elders like to tell us just to spook us. Such as a crow being a sign of death, you know that one right? I saw three in one day over a year ago and Eira nearly killed me herself when I told her just because of how paranoid she was that I was going to die and possibly take someone with me. I'm still here though, aren't I? Maybe it's just me, but I'd trust Ringwaldr's visions. He's never led me astray." Staring into her eyes with a certain look was his way of trying to reassure Echo. When Kaapo was being serious about something he meant business. Most of the time he was a flippant trickster, but he knew when to tone it down. It didn't seem to convince Echo though. She was still visibly uncomfortable and sighed to prove it.

"Well, I guess it doesn't matter whether it's a warning or not, I have to do what I'm told to, right?" Echo snapped angrily at him and got up from her chair and stormed out the front door. When Hanuel noticed she was heading for the door he very quickly followed her.

"Goodnight Kaapo, be well." The young man said in a rush then nodded to his friend before closing the door behind him.

The night had come and the air was crisp and cool. A small number of torch lights lit the path that intertwined between several cabins of the tribe. Just a few feet from the door Echo stood with her arms crossed over her chest. She caught herself, for the second time, staring at the place where the little boy had called from earlier to get her to join his game. A horrible feeling erupted in her stomach. There was no more time for games. Her parents had made sure of that. Tomorrow she had to be ready for anything, even if nothing happened on the scouting she had to be ready for the worst.

"Can I walk you to your cabin, Miss?" Hanuel said softly from behind her. Echo looked to him with sad eyes but couldn't help but smile.

"Only if you promise to be the first one waiting for me outside of it before sunrise of the scouting. Tomorrow, I'll round up scouts and meet you at the lake, but the day of, I need you here first thing." Echo said, and Hanuel's eyes widened.

"Oof, I don't know. That's a lot to ask, my friend." He said, trying to look as if he were going to disappoint her. She knew him too well though and pouted up at him as she had earlier in the forest to try and win him over. The pout made him smirk, and he wrapped his arm around her shoulders.

"Fine. It's a promise."

The two walked in silence to Echo's cabin. Hanuel gave her a reassuring pat on the back before she walked through her door, noticing she was utterly distracted by her spiralling thoughts. Then the boy left for his family's cabin to catch what little sleep he could.

3
THE VISIONS

Within the Hemera tribe there was a certain standard among its people. Yes, there were leaders, warriors, and common labourers, but the one thing that everyone believed in profoundly was that no one person was greater than the others, even if one person did have the strength of one hundred men. The standard among the Hemera tribe was that everyone had their own family cabin, and the necessities to live, nothing more or less. The leaders of the tribe, Asmund and Takoda, shared one and had given their children Echo and Kaapo their own. The reason they had given separate cabins to their children was to teach them independence and give them their own privacy so they could one day start their own families. Their true intent was a little more cunning.

THE FIRST ECHO

As a leader, there are times when you don't want your children to know what your decisions are. Not because Asmund ever thought his children would get in the way, but mostly because he didn't want them to think any less of him as a person.

"And you're sure that we are going to be the ones to initiate a battle? When there is one?" Asmund asked Ringwaldr for the thirteenth time that night.

Once Takoda, Asmund, and Ringwaldr had left Kaapo's cabin, they had agreed to split up for a short time, then meet again later that night in the seer's cabin. Ringwaldr quickly sent out a messenger to Iivona before the two leaders arrived with a low knock on his door. Avila, Ringwaldr's willowy young seer in training, answered the door and let them in. Then she took post in the corner of the stronghold. The three adults sat in a dimly lit cabin at a table with a large wooden map set atop it. The flame of the few candles placed on the table danced delicately, lighting up the map of Providence perfectly, and partially casting light on the colourful tapestries strewn over the walls. There were a total of four tapestries, each of them filled with many colours and strange symbols from different lands. There was one from The Dead Lock Mountains, another from Iivona, one from a desert city that no one but Ringwaldr understood the writing of, and lastly, Hemera's. Ringwaldr had collected them on his journey to Hemera where he finally stayed because it was the only place where his foresight had been revered, and not dreaded.

"Yes, in all of my visions Iivona does not strike first, they attempt a capture to spook us, but they do not hurt anyone." Ringwaldr reassured Asmund.

"Capture?"

"I see three...possibly four women taken, but it's hard to make out the faces." Ringwaldr squinted as if he were trying to make out a picture on the wall as he searched through his mind's eye.

"How do we prevent it?" Takoda asked worriedly.

"Everything in my bones tells me that we cannot. If we intervene, there will be death. If we let them be captured, I see a reunion."

"And you're sure you haven't seen Echo?"

"Asmund, we've been over this several times a day. The minute I see something you will be the first to know."

"That goes for me as well." Avila chimed in from her corner where she'd been silent for most of the night. Boredom got the best of her and her black eyes darted around for a chance to join in on the conversation as she played with her long, raven hair. She was taller than most women and had a look about her that would make anyone question her motives. With the power of foresight, the story was that she had sought out Ringwaldr when he passed through her village.

At the time she was living near The Dead Lock Mountains that were south of Hemera, in a small tribe that had no acceptance or understanding of the special ability she had started exhibiting at the age of twelve. Ringwaldr took her under his wing immediately and now the two were inseparable. It was a strange sort of relationship. Most of the time it had the dynamics of a father and daughter, and sometimes the roles would switch, and she'd be more of a mother to a son.

"And your visions have shown you that this scouting will go as planned?" Asmund was getting repetitive, and Ringwaldr was becoming visually agitated.

"Yes, Asmund."

The back and forth of the four adults continued until the long night finally ended. Dawn gracefully arrived in slim brush strokes of vibrant pink and orange. It had been a long sleepless night doomed into what would be the beginning of an unpleasant few days for everyone in the tribe according to Ringwaldr's visions. Around and around the four adults had gone, teetering the spokes on the wheel of possibilities. One vision led to another, and then another, and Asmund's questioning led to more questions about the same probability. They finally gave up and were left wondering what other possibilities they had missed. The two leaders left Ringwaldr's cabin and made sure to steer clear of their daughter who was undoubtedly awake and getting scouts together as the two were only now going off to sleep.

In the morning, it was easy enough for Echo to wake up because she hadn't slept very much. She spent most of the night overthinking everything about the next day's events. When everyone met at the pit for breakfast, she went around to find the scouts she wanted to take with her on the scouting and asked them to meet up at the lake when they finished. As she made her way down to the lake, she noticed the first one there was Hanuel, and she tiredly grinned over at her friend when he stood the moment he saw her coming.

"Wait, where is everyone? You didn't scare them away already did you?" Hanuel asked. Echo frowned at the joke and shook her head.

"They're coming... hopefully." She shrugged and took a seat on the log Hanuel had stood up from. Hanuel took a seat next to her and rested his elbow on her shoulder as he let out a sigh. She was far too pessimistic for him right now, and even though he'd become accustomed to it, he wasn't one to let it keep going.

"Come on. You can't sulk about this the whole time." Hanuel said, and Echo scoffed.

"Watch me." She answered with a small smirk, and Hanuel let out a short laugh and shook his head at her persistence.

"All right, we're here, tell us why Jillik and I have to miss a day of hunting for this." Manson, a fellow scout, asked as he approached with two other scouts behind him, his brother Jillik, and Saveria. Echo quickly got to her feet. Even though it was just a small group of people, she'd never been good at demanding things of others or speaking in front of groups. This was one of those times where she had to learn to be a leader. Swallowing her nerves, she waited until everyone had settled and she cleared her throat awkwardly.

"So… the seer has told my family that Iivona may be planning an attack on Hemera. The five of us have to be ready to leave by tomorrow at sunrise. We have a deep trek into the sacred forest. We must set up post a mile away from the boundary line of Iivona. We're going to watch for any signs of armed tribesmen. If we see anything, we must alert our tribe with fire, and have a runner get back. I've chosen the lot of you because… um, I was told to, and I guess… you're not half bad." Echo smirked and shrugged at the group of individuals in front of her. In turn, they looked back at her in confusion.

It was a strange looking bunch with even stranger abilities. There was Hanuel, of course, the sixteen-year-old, big-eared, young man with a mess of curls on his head who'd been her friend for as long as she could remember. Sometimes when she looked at him, she'd still see him as a round-faced boy. Through the years the shape of his face had sharpened, and somehow, he became taller than her when they had been the same height as each other for so long. He was another prodigy in their clan like her brother when it came to abilities. He could hear just about anything from miles away and see things even in the dead of night.

Next to him stood Manson, the same age as Hanuel and just a few inches shorter than him. Manson was a bit stockier and built to run. With long, dark brown hair he kept in a braid and weather-beaten skin. He was first a messenger within the tribe because of his immense speed, but he opted to be a scout because his best friend, Hanuel, had asked him. If there was going to be an emergency, he'd get back to Hemera the fastest. There was also Manson's identical twin brother, Jillik, who stood beside him. They were duplicates in every way and the only thing that gave anyone any clue of which twin they were speaking to was Jillik's forearms that were marked with black ink; tattoos that looked like roots started from his wrists and went up to his elbows. He had a very unusual ability that only one other person in his family had before him. When the young man touched the earth he could feel the spirits running through it, and sense any animal or human within a certain radius. As strange as it was it was quite useful for a scout and a hunter chasing prey. The twins were the perfect hunting duo when they were together.

On the other side of Jillik stood Saveria, an older girl by three years, with long, wavy, black hair and very dark auburn eyes. She was the same size as Echo, short and slightly curvy. Saveria was a fire bringer with a very calm temperament but a peevish personality. Kaapo used to like Saveria, and in that time Echo and Saveria became friends. Even after Kaapo and Saveria decided not to be together anymore Echo still looked up to her like an older sister. All three of the males wore the same dark tan-coloured buckskin shorts and were mostly shirtless except for their leather armour plates that hung over their shoulders. For this trek in particular they were all required to wear buckskin capes on top of that to make them blend in with the forest. The two females wore the same sort of bottoms and a twist-band halter. They had the same armour, and camouflaged buckskin capes as the boys.

After some time of the group asking questions and Echo tiredly answering all that she knew, which wasn't much, they dispersed. Echo headed off to check on Kaapo as Hanuel followed close behind. Before entering his cabin she knocked three times and Kaapo beckoned them both in with a grunt. The two took to the same positions they had the previous night while talking to Kaapo and he looked from Hanuel to his sister. The young man looked plagued by insomnia. His eyes were puffy and his face painted with pain.

"Did you get any rest brother?"

"Plenty, if you consider thrashing around and reopening a wound *rest*."

"Should I call Eira for you?" Hanuel offered and Kaapo was quick to decline.

"No she'll just wash me with more of that awful astringent and I'm not in the mood right now," he confessed. All joking was aside for him today. Truth be told, it was the first day in many years that Kaapo seemed to not want to joke around.

"Well, if you're feeling up to it, would you help me make this blade? I'd like to have it before I go on this scout, you know, just in case I run into a mob that Ringwaldr is so sure I won't." Rummaging through her shoulder pack, Echo grabbed the antler and pulled it out along with the very sharp rock Hanuel and she had picked up from the forest floor. Along with that she pulled out some of the tendrils she'd grabbed in the forest the other day. Scoffing, Kaapo threw the rock behind his shoulder, and Echo gaped at him in disbelief. He reached over to the side table by his bed, grabbing a piece of sharp iron and his own knife. Echo raised her brows, impressed that he even had that handy.

"What did you think you were going to kill with that? Next time you need the head of a blade, you come to me, and I'll ask Vult for metal from the mines." Echo gulped down when he had said the word kill. She never really thought about killing anything with it. Mainly she just needed it to scare any threats away.

"Hey, wait a minute, I told you to stop searching around there, it's still dangerous." Realizing what her brother had said her overprotectiveness kicked in. Her brother scoffed at the concern.

"Life is dangerous, get used to it Echo." Kaapo mumbled, and she responded by rolling her eyes. Before the siblings were born, there was a cave-in at the only mines that Hemera owned. The primary mine was home to many minerals that made it possible for them to have iron and steel tools. The sudden cave-in restricted the number of minerals that Hemera could mine. It became difficult for anyone to get metal, even for the children of a tribe's leader. Hemera rule made sure that the healer and army had all the metal they needed before anyone else in Hemera. From that day on, there were only a few days a year when miners would be sent to the mines to collect materials.

Unlike Hemera's counterpart Iivona, who have so

much steel that every man of their land is blanketed in armour. Asmund, and the leader before him realized that even without steel armour, their army was strong enough to take on any threat that came their way. They had proven themselves many times before with leather armour, and it was now their way of life. While Echo was caught up in her thoughts, she noticed Kaapo was carving a shape into the antler with his own knife.

"Eira really broke this well huh? It's the perfect piece to fit in your hand." He breathed as he carved out a piece in the antler to place the blade into. When he was satisfied with the notch, he began threading the tendril around the antler and the metal shard, then cut the excess of the tendril with his own knife. When he was finished he flung it at the wall across from his bed. It stuck and he nodded approvingly.

"Works well."

"Looks like it." Echo walked over to the wall, yanked the knife out and put it in the sheath around her calf.

The three of them talked for a bit before Hanuel and Echo decided to meet up with their scouting group to prepare supplies for the next day. They figured they'd give Kaapo some time to try and sleep. The entire day they were outside collecting food and supplies, dark clouds were rolling in over Hemera, threatening a storm that would only come at the most inconvenient of times.

There was a light trickle of rain, but Echo believed it was holding out its heavy downpour for tomorrow's travels. Everyone had to take non-perishables with them, and canteens for water. Aside from the survival necessities, each of the scouts were required to carry concealed weapons. Hanuel, Jillik, and Saveria carried throwing knives, Echo her new blade, and Manson preferred to carry a bow. The group was finally ready by sunset and were discussing their plan of action over dinner. Silently, Echo slipped off to bed when everyone was preoccupied talking amongst themselves.

Cold
The air was cold as ice.
Ringwaldr stood in the middle of a vast field.
The silence was numbing.
He could see nothing but his breath in front of him and the stars overhead.
The world around him began to move at a faster pace.
Amazed, he watched as the moon and stars quickly flew to the west and fell into the earth.
The sun rose an inch above the East and sat there.
Still.
As if the sun itself were waiting for something.
Ringwaldr felt a chill creep slowly up his spine.
Damp
Battle cries could be heard from a distance.
Ringwaldr set his eyes on the direction they were coming from.
From the trees erupted a sea of men riding horses as they

thrust torches in the air.
The fire flew through the air and connected with housing
he'd seen before but couldn't place.

Drowning
Ringwaldr looked behind him to set his eyes upon the
houses engulfed in flames.
From the fray, emerged another army, familiar faces
surrounded him but there were too many for him to make
them out.
He started to gasp for air, and his eyes rolled back inside
his head.
The faces of the army defending the strongholds were lost.

"Time's up!"

An annoyingly familiar voice resounded through his mind. Two scrawny hands suddenly heaved him from the waters he was drowning in and placed him sloppily at the side of the pool. Sights and sounds were cloudy as he came out of his daze. Slowly the trees that surrounded the clearing of the pool, and a light mist in the air that was lit by torches, started to come into view. The sound of the rushing waterfall played like a harmony to the heavy heart beat he could hear in his ears as percussion. When he was fully immersed in the present again and not the foresight, he began coughing up water as he snapped upright in place.

"Avila! How many times must I tell you to not wake me from a vision!" he barked. The girl rolled her eyes, as she had already anticipated he may react like this.

"Aside from the fact that I saved you from drowning, your little heiress is on the other side of the pool with her eyes closed. She's either lost her mind and trying to kill herself or she is sleepwalking." Avila pointed across the waters and there stood Echo, swaying at the edge of the pool. Ringwaldr squinted, brushing the water off of his brow and out of his eyes to get a better look at her.

"Echo!" He called out the instant before she raised a foot over the edge of the water, her other foot was barely steadying itself on the jagged stones that lined it. His voice wasn't enough to stop her. Echo's body disappeared into the water in an instant. Avila leapt to her feet and raced to the other side of the pool. She got there just in time to pull her up before Echo drifted underneath the rushing water of the falls.

"That's two lives owed to me today!" she snarled as Echo gasped for air in her arms. Ringwaldr followed Avila close behind and knelt down to meet Echo's eyes with his. She seemed bewildered, frantic even.

"Echo? What's the last thing you remember?" he asked softly. The tone was out of character for him so much so it almost seemed forced.

"I- I was in bed, then, suddenly, I don't remember how I got here."

"You have a past of sleepwalking, correct?"

"I- when I was- a child... yes." Echo's breathing and speech slowed down as she came to a disappointing realization.

This had happened to her before when she was young. She never knew why. When she drifted into sleep she'd find herself some mornings behind someone else's cabin, and sometimes at the foot of the forest. She'd never travelled this far while asleep. Eira had warned her of her sleepwalking possibly getting her into this type of trouble before but Echo had stopped tying herself to her cot when she thought she had grown out of it. Of course, Eira hadn't called it sleepwalking, Eira called it 'deadwalking'. The elders of Hemera believed profoundly in dreams and having dreams that led you places was rare amongst their people. They somehow came to the wild conclusion that 'sleepwalking' was the dead trying to communicate with you. It disturbed Echo as a child when Eira would describe it like that, and this brush with death brought back that terrible memory.

Echo got to her feet and bolted out of the forest to the path of cabins.

"You know, I'm never saving a life again, it's a thankless job." Avila said and got a fur from the edge of the pool to dry off her arms, where she'd pulled the drowning Ringwaldr from only moments ago.

"Yes, thank you Avila for saving me from a vision I've been trying to see clearly for the past three months. Really, you should be rewarded with a feast." Ringwaldr retorted sardonically. Avila sighed and shook her head at the man's irritable temper.

"I should go ask if she's all right," Avila added as she carelessly threw her towel at Ringwaldr. The man didn't answer, catching the towel and shaking his head as the young woman headed into the forest with a lit torch in her hand.

✖

In the dead of night Echo deliriously jogged down the path of the forest back to the cabins. She knew the path well enough to not need light, but it was still debilitating without it. As her eyes adjusted to the darkness, she saw the torches that lit the cabins path in the distance. When she heard the crack of a branch behind her she swivelled around to see if someone had followed her.

Amongst the trees she saw a green light like a haze quickly fall away, and it made the hairs on the back of her neck stand on end. Was something following her? Or was it a trick of the mind? The last day's events had her questioning her sanity.

Without thinking about it too much, she ran to Eira's hut knowing the woman would most definitely scold her for waking her up in the middle of the night. But Echo didn't care, she needed help. Maybe she just needed someone to snap her out of it. Echo pounded on the door twice and waited. The chattering of her teeth was all she could think about, only now realizing how underdressed she was for the cool night air and the unexpected dive in the pool. She wore a short sort of gown that was visibly tattered and very old, made of mostly buckskin.

The door swung open at a speed Echo didn't know Eira to possess and the old woman squinted up at the girl.

"What in this entire forest could you possibly need from me at this time of night?" Eira breathed. It seemed she didn't have the energy to scowl at the girl, so she just blinked at her through tired eyes.

"I'm sleepwalking again and it made me walk into the sacred pool, and I think something is following me in the forest." Echo rambled on and slipped past the old woman to sprawl herself across the bed Eira had laid out for her patients.

Eira turned to look at Echo from the door and sighed deeply as she closed it. Heavy feet shuffled across the creaky wooden floor until Eira set herself down in the wooden chair by the bed. Eira ran a hand through her hair as she opened her mouth to speak but stopped herself. Echo looked up at her with a furrowed brow.

"I'm sorry for barging in at the dead of night. I'm just… frustrated." Echo said softly. Eira looked to the other end of the room trying not to make eye contact with the girl.

"Child, I always feared you would have a difficult time with growing. I never once thought it would be this difficult for you."

"Why would you think that?" Echo's face scrunched up in confusion.

"I don't know if I should be the one to tell you this, but it may help you understand… the moment your mother went into labour with you, she made the trek to the sacred pools to birth you in its waters, as all mothers from our tribe do," Eira began cautiously. "That night there was a terrible storm. She almost didn't make it up. Your father had to carry your mother the rest of the way. Her feet left the soil on the journey. As you may remember, that is a bad sign in our tribe." Annoyed, Echo sighed deeply about the legends and old folklore from her tribe - things that people of Echo's generation treated as superstition but the older generation such as Eira treated as fact. Echo got to her feet and started pacing back and forth from one end of the small cabin to the other, a small distance to travel for her unfurling mind.

"Eira, I just want a solution. I don't want to hear about some mystical curse I have and that's the reason why I 'deadwalk' or why I'm so moody, or why I don't have special abilities."

"Your mother almost died giving birth to you Echo." Echo stopped in her tracks and looked at Eira as if she were a big kid who had just stolen a toy from a small vulnerable child.

"What? Why didn't my mother or father ever tell me that?" Echo asked angrily, but very quickly calmed herself when she realized she was directing too much anger at the wrong person.

"They've never told anyone, I only know because I had to heal her. They knew it would cause a lot of distress within our tribe to know one of the leaders' heirs did not have a perfect birth."

"This is ridiculous! What does this have to do with anything? How does the ground my mother walks on have anything to do with me?" Echo lost her temper again this time not caring who it was directed at. She had many reasons to be angry.

"Don't get snappy with me child. Know your place. Rituals and the earth around you have everything to do with your well-being. If someone kills the earth forty footsteps away from you, you think that does not affect you in any way? Stop being so naive and listen to me for once! Everything! Everything is connected! Does the existence of Jillik not set that in stone in your mind? The child touches the earth and suddenly knows where humans and animals are around him. He can sense their spirits because we're all connected. It's an incredible gift and it should teach you a lot about the earth you walk on!" It was the first time Eira had ever really raised her voice to Echo, but immediately Echo stuck her tail in between her legs and sat back down on the bed, exasperated. She didn't want to fight with the woman. That was never her intention. She just wanted answers that she was giving her but Echo didn't seem to comprehend.

"It wasn't by accident that you found the antler my dear girl. Every Hemeran of this tribe is connected to that sacred forest we are born in, in some way or another. The animals in that forest nourish us in many ways. If not by food, they teach us how to be. They give us their gifts. Your brother has the gift of the wild sigoon, your father has the strength of the great mountain bear, and your mother has the beautiful blossom of the sprints. I think that antler has come to you because you are finally coming into your abilities...

even after just a short trip in the forest." Eira raised both her brows at the girl and offered her a goblet of water she'd poured as she spoke. Echo took it from her gently and took a swig of it as she was deep in thought.

"So, you think that... I'm connected to a Hirzla?" Echo spoke softly now. Her anger dissipated and all that was left was confusion. The people of her tribe had many beliefs and one of the many was that the animals of the sacred forest were the very animals giving them their special abilities.

"I'm no seer darling, but it doesn't take a master of foresight to see when history is repeating itself right in front of them... even for a blind ol' gal like me." Shaking her head, the woman finished off her goblet and set it down on the table. Repeating itself? What history? Echo felt like prying more out of Eira, but seeing how tired the old woman was, she figured it was time to stop pressing the issue and let her be. A knock at the front door quickly took her out of her thoughts.

"Is the dead of night the new dawn? What is happening now?" Eira breathed and walked over to the door. When she opened it Avila stood there with her torch in hand, and peeked in to see Echo.

"Avila? Something wrong?"

"Sorry Eira, was just checking on our little heiress here. I pulled her out of the pools and wanted to make sure she was all right." Echo looked embarrassed at her feet, but was thankful Avila had come to check on her. Eira squinted over at Echo, only now really taking in that she was drenched with water. The old woman's eyes widened.

"Oh dear, I hadn't even noticed she was drenched… my sight really is fleeting… nevertheless, Echo's fine. She's in good hands. Thank you." Eira nodded to her and Avila nodded back, flashing a small smile to Echo before she left. Echo sighed heavily and told Eira she'd be leaving, too. Before she ran off, Eira threw a fur over her to keep her warm. Echo thanked her and headed out. It was late and she didn't want anyone else to have to deal with her turmoil at this hour of the night.

4
THE MARE'S NEST

A bird with a very distinctive whistle chirped in the distance and Hanuel sat on Echo's front stoop trying to replicate it for a few moments before Echo emerged from her door. The young man got to his feet immediately, his lanky stature rising only a foot above her. Echo gave him a weary look that seemed like she was trying to smile but turned out to be more like straining her face. He could tell she hadn't slept very well. It was written in the lines around her squinting morning eyes.

"So, I kept my promise. Do I get a prize?" Hanuel joked as he nudged her shoulder with his. Echo seemed completely out of it and ran back into her cabin to grab her satchel. After she got it Hanuel noticed her hair was stuck in the satchel's strap and quickly fixed it for her as she closed her door.

THE FIRST ECHO

"You didn't get any sleep, that's evident. Did you spend the night fighting a wild beast instead... or?" Hanuel asked with a raised brow and a grin. Echo gave him side-eye as she adjusted the satchel on her shoulder.

"I'm sleepwalking again," she mumbled. "I'll be fine," Echo added before Hanuel could say something. She noticed his face changed to a concerned look. "Let's go get the others and get going." Hanuel frowned and tried to hide his worry before continuing.

"Don't need to stop at anyone's first? Like Kaapo's or Eira's?"

"No we'll let him sleep and I don't think Eira is too fond of me right now either." As the two were walking Hanuel looked confusedly from Echo back to Eira's cabin door.

"Did you fight with the old lady while you were sleepwalking?" Echo snorted and shoved him with an open palm.

"No, you fool but I did wake her in the middle of the night when I realized I had done it. It wasn't the greatest conversation, but she gave me some things to think about."

"Oh, like what?" He asked. Echo bit her lip for a moment, unsure of how to start.

"You know how your ability makes you hear and see like a bloodhound? Well, of course, you know that..." Echo added awkwardly and shook her head at her dimness as Hanuel held back a laugh.

"I'll let you get to your point. I know you're still asleep." Hanuel smirked, and Echo rolled her eyes at herself before continuing.

"Eira thinks that maybe I have a connection to the Hirzla and that's why I found the antler. Maybe I might start noticing some ability that it has?" Completely unsure of herself or what she was saying, Echo quickly shook her head and sighed.

"Well, there's only one problem with that," he frowned. "No one really knows what the Hirzla can do. No hunter's actually caught one. Our people have only ever seen them as a warning sign, like when Draviden told everyone a Hirzla led him to the people trapped in the cave. They're so..."

"Hurry up! It's already sunrise. We should've left when it was dark!" Manson called out to them as the pair neared the entrance to the forest. It seemed their scouting group had been years ahead of them in preparedness and were already itching to leave. Manson stood at the edge of the forest with the two other scouts, his brother Jillik, and Saveria.

"Give me a break Manson, you know I've got to do my stretches in the morning or I tense up." Hanuel started flexing his somewhat lean body in ridiculous ways as he led the group into the forest. They laughed lightly as they followed behind him and the group started chatting about everything and anything to pass the time. Echo stayed quiet and withdrawn, which was normal to a degree. Usually, she'd have a sardonic comment now and then for Hanuel's antics but it was clear that she just wasn't in the right mood. A few hours later, the noon sun shone brighter through the trees, that was Echo's sign to stop and take a break. The group still had a long way to the border and she knew everyone would want to rest soon.

"Let's take a breather. The wall won't get any further if we sit down for a little while," she mumbled. Hanuel decided he was fed up with her sulking.

"I don't really need a break, but I do know who needs a swim!" The young man proclaimed before running at her and picking Echo up over his shoulder. Squealing, Echo couldn't help but let out a laugh as she asked for him to put her down. In the process she dropped her satchel while she grasped at his back to steady herself. As she struggled, Hanuel took her over to a pond and waded into it with her still very much on his shoulder. At once she broke free from his grasp but only because he decided to throw her into the water. She groaned as she plopped into the water becoming wet from the ribs down. The groan sounded very disingenuous though, considering she was smiling when she did it.

"Come on, what was that for?" Echo whined and pushed at his chest to try and get him to move out of the way so she could get out of the water she was so suddenly introduced to.

"I think you know why you sour berry! I don't want to have to scout this dumb forest with someone who looks like they're plotting to kill me." Echo cut off Hanuel with a mocking laugh.

"So you thought it was a good idea to throw that person in the water..."

"I wasn't finished!" Hanuel shot back as he cupped

Echo's cheeks in his hands, squishing them just enough so that she couldn't keep talking. By this time, the three others had caught up to the commotion and were smirking, talking lowly about the two in the water as they stood by the side of the pond.

"Oh wait, I think I was finished. I just wanted to get you to laugh." Coming to his realization he gave Echo a quick tap on the cheeks with both of his hands that held them together, then he grabbed her hand and ran out of the pond dragging her behind him.

Before she could attest Hanuel pulled Echo to him for a hug. Seemingly stunned Echo went from annoyed to being comforted fairly quickly. This was a new feeling. Sure, Hanuel was her friend. They'd hugged before. They'd been friends since they were children. They practically spent every day together, and lately, she'd noticed the kind of attention he was giving her. Her mother had told her before that boys would be looking at her differently at this age, but she never thought one of those boys would be Hanuel.

Echo suddenly became nervous at the thought of being this close to him, and she couldn't tell whether that was a good or bad thing. Before letting her go, Hanuel gave her an extra squeeze as if he was silently telling her that everything was going to be okay. Her face softened. What had been burdening her all morning suddenly felt far away in the back of her mind rather than in front of it like it had been. Manson held out Echo's pack to her with a raised brow.

"You know Hanuel, I can understand wanting

to take a bath with a pretty girl like Echo, but if you needed one you should've done that before we left."

"Don't make me pull you in too Manson. You're not half bad looking either." With Hanuel's smirk and wink, Manson's smug attitude suddenly vanished and he looked tiredly over at Hanuel.

"All right, enough games. We're losing focus. Let's rest like Echo said, and get right back on track. Have you heard anything in the distance we should be concerned about?" Hanuel shook his head no, simultaneously shaking a little bit of water out of his curls.

"Good, I need a swim too," Saveria let out in relief and dropped her things on the side of the pond before hopping into it. Jillik and Manson sat on a nearby log and everyone took a seat to relax for a short time.

The five started on their trek again. This time everyone was chattering. Jillik joked about Hanuel's true calling of becoming a fish as he runs to water like Saveria had lit a fire underneath him. Everyone got in on teasing him. Before night fell, the group set up camp in a small clearing. The twin brothers Manson and Jillik collected firewood, and Hanuel helped them build it up. When they were ready Saveria lit it with a simple wave of her hand. A small flame caught the logs and it grew from there. The girls had gotten talking, and now Echo was braiding Saveria's hair in an intricate style as they sat comfortably by the fire after they'd eaten their dinner.

When everyone was getting tired, Echo and Saveria

offered to keep first watch. The three young men sat by the fire talking low and the two girls went up the nearest tree to hold post. Before Hanuel drifted off to sleep he waved up in the trees at the two girls and sprawled himself out next to the fire, resting his head on his hand and looking up at the stars as he drifted to sleep. Saveria cleared her throat and looked to Echo.

"So... when are you two going to smash your faces together and call it a day?" Saveria giggled mischievously. Echo turned away from Saveria to hide the red that had flushed into her cheeks.

"I understand what you're getting at but I don't really have the—"

"Experience?" Saveria shot smugly.

"No... I was going to say... time... I guess..." Echo answered and it seemed she was genuinely embarrassed now because even though she wasn't going to admit she was inexperienced with any sort of intimacy, it was slowly coming to her that intimacy would become a problem for her as well.

"Aw, Echo I'm only playing with you, and why do you think you don't have the *time?* We have a good three days of scouting, I'm sure you can get in a quick peck at some point." Echo went to say something but Saveria wasn't finished. "If I'm being honest, I'm asking you to just kiss the man because I have a bet against Manson that you will finally do it, and I'd like to win against him at some point," Saveria teased. Echo felt funny, as if someone had cut a hole into a net of ten or more butterflies sitting in the pit of her stomach. She pictured herself clumsily trying to catch them all with the same broken net.

"I-I have to focus on myself right now... I'm already a late bloomer when it comes to abilities, and I've been given a responsibility that isn't supposed to be mine. My brother would probably be the one on this scout. He's always my parent's first choice for anything," Echo rambled on. Saveria's expression changed from a mischievous child to a concerned friend.

"Listen, Echo, you need to learn how to let your instincts kick in. You're very methodical, always caught up in here." The girl tapped on Echo's forehead and gave her a small grin. "I'm not saying I'm a master like Eira is with her healing, but I'm fairly good at fire bringing, and the only reason that is, is because I just...let it happen. You know? I don't think about it, I just say I'm going to do it in my head and I do it. I never do it as well as I think I'm going to...but it gets done." The girl shrugged and looked up at the stars, seemingly pleased with her explanation even though it had completely confused Echo.

"You just...do it, huh?" Echo sighed, and looked down at her swinging feet from the branch. "What if I don't know what *it* is?" she added, scrunching up her face in confusion. Saveria rolled her neck, and shrugged her shoulders flippantly.

"No one knows what it is. I didn't at first and I don't mean this in a bad way, but maybe you just have to live life with your natural abilities. Why not focus on that rather than on something that may never come?

There's a lot of great people in our tribe who still make something of themselves without abilities from the sacred animals of the forest. I think you kind of put it in your head that everyone thinks less of you for not having any...but that's not the case really." Saveria shifted on the tree branch so her head was resting on the tree's trunk, and swung her legs up to stretch them out and cross them. She nudged Echo with the top of her foot and gave her a small half-smile before looking back up at the stars. As much as Echo didn't want to hear it, Saveria was telling Echo the truth.

Saveria was right. There were people in Hemera without extraordinary abilities. There were people just surviving, just being. Maybe Echo was just one of those people, born into the wrong family. It's just that her expectations felt extremely high, and she didn't want to have to get used to that. The realization gave her a sinking feeling in her gut, and she sighed heavily before stretching out to reach for a higher branch on the tree. Echo went to the tallest branch where she could still sit comfortably, but now she was further away from Saveria and very far from the boys on the ground. Further from the ground felt better. The wind whistled through her hair and she breathed the night in deeply.

From where she was sitting she could now see the blanket of stars clearly and Saveria had started to let her small sparks of fire illuminate the clearing. They were like shooting stars that flew through the air and diminished before they hit the ground. It was a useful trick for seeing at night when they didn't have Hanuel's sight.

Climbing was when Echo felt best. Climbing away from a world where she felt she didn't belong always felt nicer than being trapped on its surface. This is where Echo would stay until later in the night when Hanuel and Jillik decided to take the next watch. No one exchanged words when they switched places because everyone was too tired. Once the morning light rolled in and everyone had slept, the group was on their way again.

The second day was quieter amongst the scouts. Everyone was tired of small talk, and now they seemed a little more fed up with walking than they had been yesterday. They made their regular stop in the middle of the day and refilled their canteens at a nearby river. Echo knelt beside it filling her canteen when Jillik decided to sit next to her and stare at her in an odd manner. The two had known each other for a while. She had a feeling he had a question. Most of the time he would ask something and leave someone to their thoughts. It was a strange phenomenon he liked to leave people with, but for some reason he still sat staring for longer than usual. It wasn't long before Echo scrunched up her face in confusion and stared back at him, but the young man still wasn't saying anything.

"Did you…need something Jillik?" Echo asked slowly. Jillik took a swig of his canteen before he answered. Manson and Jillik looked completely identical, but if you looked at Jillik long enough you could see his facial features were a bit more rounded than his twin's, softer even.

"Who do you think would win in a fight? A wild sigoon, or a bloodhound?" Jillik finally asked. Echo sighed, thinking about the question.

"I don't know, the bloodhound probably. Wigoons just know how to mimic, the bloodhound would have the senses and the speed, right?"

"Not completely true, Eira told me once they can take on an animal's ability while copying them as well."

"Well… that seems like too much power for one strange creature."

"Thanks that's how my mother describes me."

"Wait, what—"

"No time to wait, I have to ask Saveria who would win in a fight, a fire bringer or a water bringer?"

"No Jillik, wait really, I have a question now!" Echo jumped up from her kneeling position to grab Jillik by his arm and pulled him back to kneel with her before the young man tried to jump to his feet. His strange ability made Echo think about how he might be able to help her with something.

"I know you help your brother on hunts because you can feel the spirit through the ground and it's obvious that no one has ever caught a Hirzla…" Jillik stared at her impatiently. "Have you ever sensed one?"

"Hirzla? Nope. Otherwise Manson and I would've caught one by now… I mean, I don't know what I sense when I sense it, I can place it's general," Jillik waved his hand in the air spastically and Echo jumped, "shape. Like there is a map in my head. I never really know what it is." Jillik shrugged.

"And you're sure?" Echo felt like she was getting nowhere with this.

"Yes. I'm sure. You should talk to Agrun."

"Why Agrun? He doesn't really talk much… isn't he like me? He doesn't have a special ability either?"

"Yes, but he's Draviden's grandson, and *Draviden* is the only man in history who's seen one according to Eira." Jillik nodded and Echo furrowed her brow at the words. There was no harm in trying to talk to the male, but with everything going on that idea would have to wait until they were done with this scouting. After a few more seconds Echo noticed Jillik was staring at her in an odd manner again and she shrugged back at him in confusion.

"What?" Annoyed, she just wanted to know why he was staring at her like that. Jillik looked over at Saveria who gestured something to him and Jillik rolled his eyes. He sighed and finally raised his brows and started to tilt his head in the direction of Hanuel who was currently helping Manson fix his armoured chest plate. When he could tell Echo's eyes had caught Hanuel, Jillik looked wide-eyed at Echo and made kissing motions with his mouth and then shrugged. It suddenly became blatantly obvious that Jillik was trying to ask her if she was smashing faces with Hanuel without words. Of course he was in on the bet, why wouldn't he be? Echo had to give him credit. He was trying to be discreet. He couldn't just ask that question without Hanuel hearing him. Hanuel heard everything all the time. Echo rolled her eyes and swatted Jillik away. The young man took off over to Saveria, and Echo looked over at Hanuel and sighed.

"That was weird," Echo mumbled under her breath.

"Jillik's weird," Hanuel laughed as he answered Echo from afar. It was obvious he had heard the conversation the two had been having even when they were whispering. Manson looked confusedly over at his brother, and Jillik shrugged back at Manson.

As the group continued on, knowing they were nearing the wall, the chatter had finally started up again. Rather than be caught up in her thoughts, Echo contributed to some of the conversations, which were mostly friendly arguments caused by Jillik's odd questions.

The evening had finally come, and as the group was in the middle of chatting about Jillik's strange question from earlier about who would win in a fight: a bloodhound, very fast wolves with incredible sight and hearing, or a wild sigoon – a creature who could take on the form of its opponent, looking exactly alike except it didn't have pupils. All you could see were the whites of its eyes.

Hanuel suddenly heard footsteps running very hard and fast towards the group that were much different from the ones surrounding him.

Quickly, he shushed everyone and nodded to Jillik. Understanding the command Jillik nodded back and immediately stuck his hands in the dirt beneath him. The young man's eyes rolled into the back of his head for a moment.

"East of us, twenty strides or so," Jillik spat out as his eyes came back into focus. The group ran in the direction he had mentioned, weapons at the ready, and then slowly came to a halt as they realized the footsteps running towards them were coming from a boy from their tribe.

"Good, I thought you'd hear me without having to shout." Out of breath, he hunched over in relief. The boy was named Owaepo. He had dark eyes and an incredibly dark complexion. He was completely bald and his big, black eyebrows took up most of his face. Owaepo was one of the tribe's fastest messengers. Echo would bet money on the fact that the boy could keep up with the wind.

"I was sent to tell you that three of the tribe's women have been stolen. Frea, Ver, and Avila. Your father wants you to proceed with caution, and if you catch anyone coming from Iivona to head back at once. Ringwaldr requests that you capture any civilian you find."

"What?" said Saveria, instantly opposed to the idea.

"He wasn't finished," Hanuel said calmly.

"I wasn't finished!" Owaepo chirped and then looked to Hanuel embarrassed as it seems Hanuel had already made that clear for Owaepo. The young boy took another deep breath in to continue as he was still out of breath from running. "If it is too dangerous, do not attempt it. That bit was added by your mother." Owaepo knowingly looked to Echo when he said that.

"What? How do I know what is too dangerous?

Is that all they said!" Echo asked angrily. She hadn't wanted to be out here in the first place. This was never what she had signed up for. Now, there was even more being asked of her.

"That's all," Owaepo added with a shrug before breathing in deeply and taking off through the group, heading in the direction of Iivona. The group gaped in complete silence. No one dared to move. Jillik looked to Echo and gulped down.

"I've never really… captured anyone. Never had to. I know the message came from the seer but… can we agree on it being our last resort?" Without hesitation, the group nodded in agreement with Jillik. In the back of Echo's mind was Ringwaldr. There was no doubt in her mind that he had seen something, but how could he ask so much of her? Her superstition had been worked up as of late, and the fact that this request came from him made her head dizzy with paranoia. The group continued on walking, now surrounded by a completely uncomfortable silence.

Once they'd reached another small clearing, Echo noticed the sun was setting and they stopped for the evening. The boys gathered wood and started a fire. After everyone had eaten Manson and Hanuel decided to take first watch.

As night crept in, the two young men got comfortable high up in a tree beside the clearing. The moon up above shone brightly enough that they could see some of its glow through the trees but their eyes had mostly adjusted to the darkness now. There was the fire that they had lit earlier dying out beneath them, and the two girls sat beside it. Echo was mindlessly braiding Saveria's long hair into an intricate braid again. Both of them seemed quieter than the last night. Jillik had completely passed out beside the two girls after he'd eaten. Manson was sitting beside Hanuel on a branch, tossing a small pebble up and catching it out of boredom. Hanuel sighed deeply knowing everyone was still a little on edge from the messenger incident.

"I'll give you my last piece of dried elk if you can throw it past that crow's nest over there." Hanuel squinted into the night, pointing at a large branch just on the other side of the small clearing. Manson turned to Hanuel and scoffed at him. Sometimes Hanuel forgot that no one could see what the boy could see at distances especially with no light source.

"I can barely see it, and I might hit one of the girls if it ends up falling to the ground." Manson protested quietly as he gave the pebble in his hand another light toss upwards to catch it again in an instant.

"That's all right. If Echo decides to hit you I'll restrain her, and Saveria's got a lot of hair as cushioning so you won't hurt her." Hanuel smirked and gave Manson a small nudge.

The young man rolled his eyes but obliged with a spiritless shrug. He then stretched the arm with the pebble in his hand all the way behind his head before launching it towards the branch. It just tapped the branch the nest sat upon and fell back into the camp's fire, making it pop up suddenly from the movement in logs. The small pop made Saveria jump, and Echo looked around wondering what had happened. When she looked up at the two in the tree she scoffed. The young men sat dumbfounded then laughed and Hanuel handed his last piece of dried elk from his shoulder pack to his friend.

A couple of hours later Hanuel was slowly drifting in an out of sleep while Manson was completely awake, carving a piece of wood into no particular shape with the knife he'd borrowed from Hanuel. An owl hooted in the distance, making Hanuel jump slightly. He sighed tiredly to himself as he shifted on the tree to see it better. A sudden thought of Echo climbing up that tree with a brooding expression and a free hand swatting the animal away so she could sit on that higher branch made him snort. He looked down at her now sleeping by the fire. Anyone could see a look of longing in his eyes except her. Manson smirked over at him and ruffled Hanuel's hair.

"Don't worry, she'll come around someday," he teased.

Hanuel looked dumbfounded for a moment before going completely red in the face with embarrassment.

"Would you be silent. You're going to attract wolves, or worse, bloodhounds." Hanuel mumbled and Manson smirked, his smug look slowly irking Hanuel even more.

"Oh come now, the three of us have a bet that you two are going to smash faces by the end of this scouting. I'm betting against you though. I don't think you can do it." Hanuel rolled his eyes at his friend and continued staring down at Echo. He didn't mean to stare but he liked the way the campfire's light danced on her face.

"In the long run you have nothing to worry about anyway friend. Everyone knows that if your senses get stronger, you build enough muscle to become the next army leader like your father. Asmund will be begging you to take her hand in marriage."

"Oh, is that all? I just need her family to approve, not her?" Hanuel remarked sarcastically.

"Well, you know, the girl's useless regardless," Manson mumbled, and when Hanuel heard it he punched Manson square in the arm nearly making him lose his balance on the tree branch. Manson sat there shocked for a moment trying to understand why he had hit him.

"She's not useless." Hanuel spat through gritted teeth. Suddenly Manson's expression changed from shocked to apologetic.

"Oh... oh no, brother I meant as an heir. You know... there are whispers about Asmund being worried that she will not be able to keep up with Kaapo. She's a fine woman. Better at most survival skills than me, but look at it from his eyes for a moment. He's got an heir that became a Hemeran hero before any man in our history because of his talent. Then he's got a wife who's more frightening than mother nature at her worst... the gamble of them having both of their children having their sort of talents was a huge one, and from what others have said I just meant that. That is how *he* sees her... understand?" Manson finished lowly. Hanuel gave him a look from the corner of his eye but did not answer. His eyes were still focused on Echo. Manson had a point. Kaapo and Echo would be up for a vote once their parents passed on their leadership, and if the people saw her unfit, there was a great chance she wouldn't be voted in next to Kaapo. Hemera customs called for one man and woman leader of the tribe. The way Asmund gained leadership was by becoming a hero of war. Takoda was voted in when the previous female leader Lela, a shifter, died. Leaders were not changed unless they were seen unfit by the elder's council. Asmund and Takoda married after only a few years of working together, and the rest was history. A history that Hanuel learned in lessons with both of the siblings because he was the son of an army leader, he spent most of his time growing up next to the heirs of Hemera. Hanuel sighed to himself and looked back at his friend with furrowed brows.

"You could've made that clearer before I almost knocked you off the tree."

"Believe me friend, I wish I had." Manson laughed in disbelief of the pain in his shoulder as he rubbed it.

While Hanuel was still thinking about Manson's comment, something else had caught his attention.

"It's close."

He heard the delicate voice like an unwelcome guest had entered his mind. It confused him for a moment. It sounded familiar, so he looked down at both of the girls. When he noticed that neither of them had been awake he shook his head and tried to listen more intently. He didn't want to jump to conclusions, but the voice sounded like it had been close to them. He tapped Manson on the shoulder and pointed to the bow on the young man's back. Manson wielded it and waited for instruction, aiming it out into the distance of the trees just beside his sleeping friends on the ground.

"What are you hearing?" Manson whispered.

"I don't know," Hanuel said in a frustrated tone. "Stay quiet while I figure it out!"

The two sat in dead silence. The only thing Hanuel could hear were the sounds of the night amplified as he usually did. Crickets, stirring rodents, and owls hooting, the sound of moving things were dull to him now, like branches or leaves swaying in the breeze. It was easy for him to tell the difference. The voice he focused on was a woman's and now he could hear her footsteps. Unless she had six feet, it sounded like she was being followed by an animal. Or perhaps, there was an animal very close to her. He couldn't tell which way the footsteps were going, but he let his guard down a little. It seemed as if wherever the voice was going was not near them, and she wasn't in a hurry.

"It might be nothing. Someone's in the forest. The footsteps are strange." Hanuel looked down at the sleeping Jillik, wanting to wake him to see what he could sense, but also not wanting to wake up Echo in the process. It had been two nights now that she didn't sleep walk, or 'deadwalk' as Eira so famously liked to call it, and he just wanted her to get as much sleep as possible. If the footsteps seemed like they were getting very loud and close all at once, he would have to wake everyone up.

"If it's just her alone she's probably not a threat," Manson added, and Hanuel adjusted himself on the branch.

"I don't know if it's just her that's the thing... just keep your eyes open," Hanuel added as he stared into the trees.

"Shouldn't I be telling you that? Seeing as you are the one who can see the clearest at this time of night?" Hanuel yawned but never answered Manson. Only an hour later the two switched with Saveria and Jillik on the ground. Hanuel let the two know there was a woman close enough to hear, but not too close, and commanded them to keep an eye out for anything suspicious. Jillik stayed on the ground with his knife at the ready for the rest of the night while Saveria sat posted in the tree. If there was any sort of animal or person within fifty yards of them, he'd be able to sense something through the earth, so he stayed alert. Every now and again Saveria would throw sparks into the distance that would crackle through the night air illuminating the forest beyond the clearing for just a few seconds, and then disappearing before it hit the ground. She always made sure they weren't a complete fire hazard, yet Jillik held his breath every time she did it, scared that she'd suddenly light the whole forest on fire.

5
THE
STRANGER

When morning finally came, the group woke slowly and silently. No one spoke to each other as they prepared tools for a meal. When Echo took her wooden bowl of rice from Jillik, she noticed he was the only one who seemed as calm as she was. Everyone else in the group seemed a little on edge. Seeing the tension, and not understanding it, Echo nudged Saveria as she sat next to her by the fire to eat.

"Is there a reason everyone looks like they're hiding something?" Echo whispered to Saveria with a raised brow. She was mostly joking but seeing Saveria's face after she'd asked, Echo was a little frightened of what she'd say next.

"Last night Hanuel heard something in the forest. He wasn't sure if it could be a threat but we were all pretty worried about it," said Saveria, keeping her tone low. Echo didn't care to be polite at this point.

"What happened last night? Why didn't someone wake me?" Echo blurted out. The four others exchanged frightened and confused looks. Setting her glare on Hanuel, she knew he'd give her an answer. The boy gulped down what little bit of hot soup he'd put into his mouth and shrugged.

"I heard something last night in the woods. A woman's voice. I was going to tell you if it turned into something but we seem okay for now. I just didn't want to bother you with anything. You haven't been sleepwalking while we've been out here so I didn't want to disrupt you." Hanuel shrugged again, and Echo looked to her feet in a bit of shame. She didn't have a reason to be angry with him, but the potential of someone ambushing their camp and Hanuel not telling her about it the moment it happened made her a little uneasy.

"Alright let's get going then. We're close to the wall. We need to make sure we get there as quickly as possible." The four didn't argue with her even though they had been rushed through their meal. They noticed how agitated Echo had suddenly become and began to pack up their satchels with all their tools. Finally, when everyone was ready they headed off. The morning started off quietly. With the past two days' events, it was becoming apparent that this scouting was slowly getting worse by the day.

Besides that, Echo felt something itching beneath her skin. Something she never felt before and didn't know how to explain. It surprised her that she hadn't been sleepwalking on this outing. If anything she imagined she would've been called out by whoever was keeping watch during the night to wake her, but thankfully it just hadn't happened.

The group came to a stop by a small stream next to a cave. Without saying anything Echo jumped up a nearby tree and scaled her way up with ease. Nearing the top, Hanuel came over to look up at her from down below.

"That's pretty high Echo. You trying to see something?" Noticing she had to be at least twenty feet up, he shouted.

"Yeah, I wanna see how far the wall is. Maybe I can catch something," she answered back. Hanuel noticed he had heard two voices at the same time. Echo's, and the familiar voice from last night, but because he'd been listening to Echo at the same time, he couldn't make out what the other person had said. Trying with all his might to centre in on the voice, he quieted down completely.

Nothing... and then... footsteps.

Running at full speed.

Close – but which direction was indiscernible.

"Jillik!" Hanuel called out. Confused, the boy looked bewildered to him, and Hanuel pointed to the ground. Jillik's eyes went wide realizing what he was asking of him and he hit the dust. Digging his hands into the dirt as he was so accustomed to doing, his eyes rolled back into his head again. Almost instantly he turned to the direction the footsteps were running.

From twenty feet up Echo could see the forest brush moving in the distance. A red blur was flying between the flora. A woman was running. Her long, red hair flew behind her. On the ground the four took off in the direction Jillik had pointed out. Hanuel figured it would be safe enough. It was just one set of footsteps, and the girl seemed to be following his group. Reading the situation rather quickly, Echo realized she had to get to the ground. Echo made a quick reach for a branch, but her hands had different plans for her.

She missed.

Echo never missed a branch.

Not once in her life since the first time she'd started climbing at the age of six.

Before she could even think, Echo felt the rush of air through her hair.

Goosebumps erupted from her skin.

There was a sinking feeling in her stomach.

Am I falling?

In the next moment Echo was on the ground on all fours. A small gasp left her mouth. She felt a jolt in her stomach but no pain in her limbs. Quickly, she got to her feet and didn't question the moment's events as she was still in the middle of catching up to everyone.

When Echo caught up to the group she found Manson holding the girl's hands behind her back. Of course he had caught up to her, his running speed was twice the speed of anyone else's. The stranger struggled a bit in his grasp but instead of looking terrified she looked eerily calm.

"Wh-who are you?" Echo stammered out of breath. The girl's long, red hair was a bit of a mess but was still very beautifully placed on her head. Her skin was whiter than the Hemeran's that surrounded her, ghostly in fact. She wore a large black cape but Echo could tell she was sweating in it. Maybe this girl was from The Deadlock Mountains? Echo knew of one tribe there that had to survive a colder temperature all year round but it wouldn't have made sense as to why she was coming from Iivona's direction.

Echo regained her normal breathing and walked up to the girl inspecting her emotionless and murky blue eyes. A wave of familiarity hit Echo unexpectedly. The girl's face was speckled with small brown dots that Echo had only ever seen once before in her life. She vaguely remembered her mother calling them freckles when Echo had asked what they were. Walking around the girl, she noticed a mark on her wrist. A strange shape that looked like something she'd seen from her father's journals. The one he kept while he was at war with Iivona so many years ago. For the life of her, she couldn't remember where in the journal she'd seen it, but everything about this girl was too familiar for her liking. Why the girl dressed so strangely was anyone's guess. The most alarming thing about her was the burns on her hands.

Even though Echo had given the girl time to identify herself she just stood there, staring at Echo as she scanned her. With a storm of thoughts brewing in her mind Echo sighed heavily. The last thing she remembered feeling was a sickly knot in the pit of her stomach when she'd missed the branch, the cool air running through her hair, and then the solid ground beneath her. How would she even begin to explain that to anyone? She could barely explain the events to herself in her head. There wasn't a way. Now she had run into this stranger and she had to play leader because she was the daughter of one. The weight to bare here was getting to be a little too much.

"We're not going to hurt you but we need to know why you've been following us. We heard you last night in the forest."

Still no answer.

"Do you know anything of the messages of war?"

The girl smirked and a chill ran up Echo's spine. If she understood what Echo had said, maybe she just didn't know how to answer her.

"Maybe she speaks the old language? The one my father and Ringwaldr know? It's possible she doesn't know the new trading language," Echo said slowly as she looked to everyone else.

"I don't want to say it... but I think this is that last resort situation," Hanuel said slowly. Echo sighed but nodded in agreement. Everyone could see Saveria was about to protest but Echo cut her off.

"We're taking you back to Hemera. Maybe someone else can get you to talk about why you were following us." Echo gave Saveria a pointed look, and Saveria sighed heavily and exchanged a look with Jillik who was also visibly irritated with the conclusion. This must have been what Ringwaldr had seen, but it almost seemed too simple. Echo wasn't happy with the outcome either, but at this point she was in over her head, and she wanted to get back to Hemera as soon as possible. As the rest of the group exchanged uncomfortable looks, Hanuel tilted his head in confusion. Echo knew that face very well. He was hearing something else.

"Is that what I think it is?" he breathed, and suddenly looked frightened. "Everyone stay quiet, I think it's a hound," Hanuel whispered and gulped down. Jillik and Hanuel whipped out their sheathed daggers as Manson kept a firm hold on the girl. No one dared to move after they had readied themselves.

If there was one around, that meant its pack was not far behind. Bloodhounds were like coyotes with better senses. Unlike coyotes, bloodhounds were a little braver when approaching humans. Hanuel focused as much as possible on the footsteps of the creature. Quickly, they became louder and louder as the creature came closer to the group. A bloodhound's speed alone was something only Manson could keep up with but now he was holding on to the girl they had just captured.

The redhead let out a high-pitched cry that resounded like an alarm. Manson quickly covered her mouth. Jillik hit the dirt placing his hands on the ground to try and locate the animal but as he moved, the creature jumped out of the brush and almost nabbed Saveria's arm. She moved just in time, and threw a spark in its face as it tried to jump for her again. When the creature was stunned by the small burn to its nose, Jillik took a chance, and leapt on top of it as he was the closest to Saveria. The hound let out a gruesome whine as Jillik fell on top of its back legs, but somehow it managed to get away from his grasp and ran off back into the brush. The group was spooked, and honestly, waiting for more to come at them, but were surprised when all was quiet. For a moment Echo was scared that maybe the redhead was calling for more of her tribe, but it almost seemed like she was just calling out to the hound. After a minute of waiting in dead silence Hanuel let out a slow sigh of relief.

"I don't hear its breathing or footsteps anymore I think that was the only one." The group was confused, but relieved all at once. Echo looked to the girl still trapped by Manson. She hadn't seemed phased by anything that had just happened, but she was glaring at Echo for some reason.

After the incident the new group was off, this time in the direction of Hemera. It had been a short and concise conversation of heading back because of the messenger's orders and the simple fact that they didn't want another run-in with a hound. It was a good thing really. Everyone was exhausted and even though they had prepared themselves for five days and nights of scouting, it was clear that they had gotten all the action they needed out of those five days in only three.

As the group walked Echo's mind raced. If Ringwaldr had envisioned this, what else had he seen? Had he seen her fall but not really fall out of the tree?

THE FIRST ECHO

Had he seen the hound attack? Was that of such importance for him to see? Maybe it wasn't. No one really got hurt, but how did she not hurt herself when she came down from the tree? It was a great height. It must've been exhausting for him, constantly seeing the possible outcomes the future could bring, but it was even more exhausting not having any idea of what could happen next. It made Echo question everything that had happened. *Maybe I wasn't that high up in the first place? Maybe I blacked out and quickly scaled down the tree like I've done so many times before?*

Everyone seemed to be walking faster. Exhaustion and frustration fuelled their need to make it back to the tribe. The group was completely out of breath at sundown. The boys started to make a fire as the girls prepared the tools for a meal, all the while keeping an eye on the redhead who they now had tied to the nearest tree. When they realized they only had enough food for them, Echo offered to share her meal with the girl. She split up her portion of pemmican and handed the girl some as they all sat by the fire. The redhead took it without hesitation and scarfed it down. They only let her have one hand free while the other stayed tightly bound to the tree. When she finished eating, both of her hands were bound again. No words were exchanged for most of the day. It had been a long time since anyone said anything, even Hanuel, which was fairly unusual for him.

The girl made no efforts to speak to the others. Funnily enough, she seemed like the only one comfortable with the situation, even while being bound against her will. While everyone was on edge she had a look in her eyes that told Echo she completely knew what she was in for. Echo tried to shake off the stress of the day. When she had finished eating by the fire someone finally broke the long awkward silence.

"Hanuel and Echo, you're the only two who haven't held first post for the night. Get to it," Manson said, then hid his smirk as he took a swig from his canteen. The two mentioned exchanged a look, and then got to their feet. Echo found a tree near the clearing with several branches that were only a short distance away from the tree the redhead was bound to, and started her way up it.

"I hope you picked an easy one for me," Hanuel mumbled as he followed Echo up. She went to a branch just to the left and slightly above where Hanuel found a comfortable nook near the trunk.

The two exchanged a slightly awkward look then Echo smiled weakly at him before looking up at the sky through the leaves. No stars. Cloudy. That wasn't exactly a good sign. She thought they'd escaped a storm when they were given a good two days of weather after a day of rolling clouds, but the sky had caught up to them and would show them her wrath in one way or another. In the past two days everyone had been making jokes about Hanuel and Echo flirting, and now here they were, stuck together in a tree.

"I didn't do something to upset you, did I Echo?" Hanuel whispered over to her. Echo frowned at the thought of him thinking he could ever upset her.

"What? No! Not at all. I'm just upset about the situation. Everything that's going on... it's getting to be a little more than I expected...I mean I didn't expect a brisk walk in the forest, but I also wasn't prepared for a hostage and a hound," she rambled on and then let out a dramatic sigh. When she looked over at Hanuel she noticed he hadn't taken his eyes off her once. It made her nervous again. She'd never been nervous around him before this scouting.

"Is there something on my face?" she asked shyly, but also a little annoyed. If there was something he'd be the one to laugh and not tell her until she found out later and swatted him on the shoulder for letting her walk around like that.

"No, I was just listening. Didn't mean to stare," Hanuel admitted and rubbed the back of his head with his hand as his eyes darted around. Echo could tell there was something on his mind, and it made her feel selfish. All he ever did for her was listen and she appreciated the fact that he seemed to enjoy her anxious ramblings rather than get bored of them.

"Are *you* okay?" she asked him softly and the boy looked over at her with a mildly shocked expression. Quickly, he shook his head yes, but Echo could tell it wasn't very genuine.

"Come on, you're never one to be at a loss for words. Tell me what's on *your* mind for once." Echo grinned and Hanuel bit his lip.

"I guess I'm just...worried about everything, how it's

affecting you. What with how worried you were about the antler before, and now everything's gone…well, you know, badly." Hanuel knew she agreed when he saw her grin slowly fade from her face.

"I haven't stopped thinking about it to be honest," Echo replied and Hanuel nodded his head in understanding. Echo unsheathed the dagger from her leg and inspected it in her hand. Was it really a curse to carry this thing around? Or would it protect her from all of the madness that had been occurring like Eira had stated? So far it seemed that it had been the result of her having to be on this scouting instead of her brother in the first place. Echo put it back in her sheath and shook her head at the ridiculous thoughts. The two sat in a mutual silence until Hanuel opened his mouth to say more but then quickly stopped himself.

"What?" Echo asked noticing the quick change, but Hanuel shook his head in protest.

"Nothing."

"No, you were going to say something, what is it?" Echo persisted and Hanuel protested harder.

"Believe me… it's nothing." Echo furrowed her brow and grabbed his ear from her branch tugging on it and making him seethe.

"Ow, let go you! What are you? An angry sprint?" he whispered loudly, trying to not call too much attention to himself from the others below. The grip she had on his ear was easy enough to force off with his hand but he was currently using both of them to steady himself on the tree so he wouldn't fall. Echo continued to grip on just tightly enough that he couldn't escape but not hard enough that she'd hurt him too much.

"Fine, but now I'm hurt that you won't tell me," Echo responded and let go of the grip she had on his earlobe. Hanuel looked aghast.

"*You're* hurt? *You?*" He reached out to pinch the side of her stomach as he said it. She jumped and laughed at the quick movement and then shushed him to settle both of them down.

The two looked at each other and Echo noticed his cheeks had flushed with red. For a moment she thought the same thing might have happened to her. Out loud she'd never admit it, but her stomach butterflies had come back, and they put this little thought in her head of wanting to scoot over on to Hanuel's branch and find a way to sit with him where he'd have his arm around her shoulders. The thought made her gulp a little too audibly and she set her eyes to the dark clouds overhead again. Hanuel had always been someone she trusted, someone she could go to for any reason. It had suddenly become so difficult for her to tell him how she was feeling at this moment. She wanted to blame all of her friends for putting this kind of pressure on them both, but she knew it was really just her over thinking everything like she usually did.

For a long while Hanuel set his sights to the forest, catching glimpses of Echo with side glances as they sat in silence watching for any threats. The three young adults by the fire finally fell fast asleep, and the fire had completely settled down. By this time it was smouldering and that was when Hanuel seemed to build up the courage to speak again.

"You know… Manson made a bet with Saveria that I couldn't… that we would… um… how do I say this?"

Echo looked wide-eyed at him. She could feel her heart pounding in her chest the minute Hanuel said *bet*. She wasn't sure if she should answer him or let him struggle to find the words.

"They have a bet? Is Jillik in on it?" Echo asked him slowly, playing dumb.

"Well you know him, he's always betting against his brother, and yeah… they have a bet going, it's about, whether or not I will… um…"

"Whether or not you will… get whatever you're trying to say out right now?" Echo smirked and Hanuel sighed and rolled his eyes, internally deciding that he was finished struggling with the words.

"They have a bet going on whether or not we're going to… kiss by the end of this scouting, and I told Manson it was stupid. First of all he uses that phrase 'smash faces' and I don't know about you but it sounds terrible like that, and I know it's not the kind of stuff we should be thinking about right now. We should really be paying attention. I think your parents always put so much pressure on you to succeed all the ti—"

"Hanuel?" Echo said softly and Hanuel finally breathed after his long-winded nervous speech.

"Yes Echo?"

"Can you come sit beside me?"

The young man breathed in deeply and obliged

with a nod all the while trying his very best to stay composed. It was clear the two had felt closer than usual, but for some reason, were staying so far. Echo realized now that she knew what Hanuel wanted by starting this conversation. So she wanted him closer. Hanuel grabbed onto her branch from where he was sitting. As he inched closer to her, she moved so that they could sit side by side. Wrapping an arm around her shoulder he heaved a heavy sigh. Those pesky little stomach butterflies were at their old tricks again. She just couldn't control them, especially because they had just gotten their way.

The two stared out at the forest for a moment. Echo could see nothing but darkness and the redheaded girl sitting by the smoulders. Sighing, she turned to look at him and noticed he was already staring at her in the dark. She always wondered just how clearly he could see anything in the night. He'd tried to explain it to her once, but she never really understood. She flashed him a small nervous grin. Without taking his eyes off her mouth, Hanuel gently lifted her chin and moved in closer until his lips met hers. Shocked, Echo's eyes widened and then fell closed. Her heart raced as she suddenly felt dizzy, the kind of dizzy you feel when you're a kid spinning in a field until you fall into the green lush grass and stare up at the slowly swirling clouds.

Echo never really thought about this moment. The idea of kissing had never occurred to her before her friends started teasing them to do it. Now that she was doing it, she felt stupid she'd never tried to kiss Hanuel before. Hanuel slowly placed his hand on her neck as his thumb traced her jawline. His fingertips caused a wave of goose bumps to travel down her arms. For a moment, she indulged in this.

However, the past two nights had proven to be the most eventful and she'd feel like an absolute imbecile if she was sitting on a branch smashing faces with her best friend when something would choose now, of all times, to go wrong. Her paranoia got the best of her and she pulled away from him. Both of them looked flushed and Echo stuttered, trying to explain why she had stopped the kiss but there was no time. Looking out at the place the redhead had been, there was no blazing red colour beneath the tree anymore.

The rope had been undone and left there.

Hanuel followed Echo's eyes to where she was looking. They both jumped into action, sliding down the tree one after the other.

"I hear her jogging, I think she's this way." Flustered, Hanuel pointed and Echo followed quickly behind him.

"Why didn't you hear her escape?" Echo asked and Hanuel scoffed.

"I was a *little* preoccupied," he shot back. "Wait, I see her!"

Echo's eyes adjusted to the dark just a little but she still couldn't see what was in front of her as she ran. She held on tightly to Hanuel's arm as he led the way with his owl sight, when suddenly he came to an abrupt stop. Echo accidentally smashed into the back of him and then looked around as she found herself in a smaller clearing. The moonlight cut through the dense clouds for a moment, and as Echo's eyes feverishly tried to adjust to the dark, she noticed the redhead only a few feet away. She paused as she had found herself stuck in front of some dense brush she couldn't pass through.

All three of the young adults froze, exchanging looks in the darkness, each one figuring out how to move first. Hanuel jumped one way as he had her in his sight, but she was too quick, and jumped the opposite way, now just a few feet from Echo. Echo felt a jolt in her stomach and jumped towards the sound of the girl's footsteps in hopes that she'd knock her down. Something in her made her move so quickly that she crashed into the redhead's side a bit too abruptly. The girl fell to the ground, completely winded and coughing. Echo looked bewildered at the girl on the ground and then all around herself.

"What is that?" Hanuel breathed hard as he stared at Echo. The air surrounding Echo seemed to hold a glowing green mist that slowly faded away, but because of the dark, Hanuel didn't know what it was exactly. Even for someone who could see in the dark, he couldn't make out something he'd never seen before this situation. Echo's skin crawled, and her heartbeat quickened. The girl on the ground let out a sinister laugh, and immediately Hanuel grabbed the redhead by the arm to pick her up. The three began to walk back to the dying fire. Hanuel dragged the girl and Echo followed behind as he was the only one who could really see the way back.

Saveria was the only one awakened by the ruckus.

"Really? You lost her?" Saveria asked in a petulant tone, half asleep, as she sat up by the now smouldering fire.

"We found her didn't we? Settle down," Hanuel shot back. This time Echo and Hanuel made sure to tie four knots rather than two around the girl's wrists. As the two did so, Saveria woke up Jillik. "She already escaped once. Don't let her do it again," Hanuel very demandingly told the two as Saveria slid up into the nearest tree and Jillik sighed, taking a seat close to the girl with his knife at the ready. Echo found she wasn't used to this serious side of Hanuel. She couldn't tell if he was angry or scared when he was like this. Hanuel took Echo gently by the arm and walked a little further away from the sleeping Manson, smirking red-head and very confused looking Jillik.

"I don't know what I just saw back there, and I think I'm too exhausted to get an explanation right now, but I need to know one thing..."

"Yes?"

"Are you... did you push me away because—"

"No."

"You seemed to not like it and I don't want to lose yo—"

"Hanuel, stop," Echo breathed, and put both of her hands on his cheeks as he had to her before in the pond when he wanted her to stop talking nonsense. It took a lot of strength not to kiss him again. Knowing that would make him feel better, but make the situation more complicated, she held back. "I only pushed you away because there's too much pressure riding on me and this scouting right now, and look how bad it's gotten already. I just don't want to screw up… again…" Shaking her head Echo looked down at her feet. "When we get back to Hemera, and figure out this mess… I would very much like to sit in a tree with you," Echo said insistently, and then smirked as she realized she still had his cheeks squished in between her hands. Hanuel flashed a small, somewhat sad kind of grin and Echo's grin slowly started to match his in the same sadness. She dropped her hands from his face and hugged him tightly around his waist. In response he wrapped his arms around her shoulders and gave her a quick kiss on the side of her forehead. The gesture made her heart hurt.

If everything wasn't so complicated, if they were just at home in their regular routines, maybe their first kiss could have gone differently. The two parted, and tried their hardest to fall asleep around the campfire. As Echo lay on one side of the pit, opposite Hanuel, she looked over the smouldering glow to see him looking back at her. She noticed he was going to have as much trouble going to sleep as she was.

The rain rudely awoke the sleeping group. It started with a light shower and then came beating down on

104

them. Thankfully they all had buckskin capes. The young redhead's black cape didn't seem so odd now even though she had been sweating in it yesterday. The stranger trudged behind the group. She was being pulled by a rope around her wrists that Manson held on to as they walked through the sludge and leaves on the forest floor. The group couldn't do much talking as they walked through the rain. The roaring sound of thunder made it feel as if the earth was quaking beneath them.

Hanuel attempted to catch some rainwater with his canteen and held it up, forgetting to watch where he stepped in the process. It was obviously a bad idea to everyone around him and he ended up tripping over a log and dropping the canteen in mud. When Manson let out a burst of laughter after witnessing the scene, Hanuel picked up his muddy canteen and threw it at him. It bounced off the side of Manson's face. That was enough to make him stop and make his brother Jillik erupt in the same laughter his brother had just ended. Saveria and Echo exchanged a short look of disappointment, and everyone was on their way once again.

Despite the bad weather they were making good time. They were close enough to home that they decided to travel through the evening without stopping for a meal, and were welcomed at the fire pit with cattle cooking on the spit.

The original group of five that was now six went straight to the leader's hut. They were met by Takoda who was taken aback by the new face. The girl was a bit startling. Her lighter skin tone was enough to show that she wasn't from Hemera, and her blazing copper hair was the first thing anyone could see.

A confused silence was amidst the air in the room, and no one said anything until Takoda decided she should.

"Welcome home. To those who return. Welcome stranger. Even though you are tied up like a prisoner, I should hope my child hasn't treated you like one," Takoda began and then turned to Echo when she became a little unsettled by the redhead's emotionless stare.

"I don't think she speaks the new language," Echo said slowly, and Takoda took it into account with a curt nod.

"All right, well, go fetch your father. He's by the carpenter's stronghold. He's been helping them build a new cabin through the bad weather," her mother said and Echo responded with a nod before heading out the door.

It was a short jog to the carpenter's cabin and when she arrived she noticed her father with a load of logs on his back. He had two, ten-feet-tall tree trunks on either side of his shoulders. Even in the onslaught of rain, he was walking them over to a pile and throwing them down with practised ease. Any regular man would struggle with one. Sometimes Echo didn't realize how shocking her father's strength really was.

He looked to her and she waved him over. Echo wondered if her life would be different if she were born into a family that wasn't leading a tribe. She imagined running and hugging her father, as if she had just gone on a short trip, and not a scouting party of war. The notion seemed useless when there was business to be discussed. Human relations became far and fickle when you had many lives to worry about. It made her wonder if she'd ever be able to enjoy Hanuel's company without the burden of a tribe over her head.

"Welcome home." Her father nodded to her and she nodded back. They both headed to the cabin. Echo was sure that when she returned, it would most likely be packed with the group of five scouts, the new stranger, her parents and Ringwaldr. She remembered Avila, and gulped down. If Avila hadn't been kidnapped by what she presumed to be the Iivona tribe she would most definitely be at Ringwaldr's side during this.

When they finally arrived at the cabin, they entered, and Echo looked around in confusion. Takoda sat at the worn-looking table with the redheaded girl across from her. Ringwaldr stood behind Takoda with his arms crossed, but everyone else from the scouting group had disappeared.

"Where is everyone?" Echo asked no one in particular.

"Didn't need them. Sit," Ringwaldr demanded, and Echo didn't appreciate the tone. Without answering, she took to the opposite side of the room to him. She crossed her arms over her chest, and it shifted the leather chest plate that hung off of her small frame. It had been passed down to her by her mother, making it even more apparent that even though she was of age, she was still a child when it came to matters like this. Echo straightened up her back and breathed out, trying to relieve her stomach's feeling of nervous nausea and the bottled hatred she had for Ringwaldr's tone towards her. Now she was in between the stranger, her mother, and Ringwaldr where she stood in place.

"Young girl, the mark on your wrist tells me you come from Iivona. What do you know of the army called forth?" Ringwaldr asked the stranger.

"I already told mother, I don't think she speaks the new language," Echo mumbled. Ringwaldr didn't look at Echo but tried the same question in the old language that Echo barely understood. The redheaded girl raised a brow and looked from Ringwaldr who had asked the question then to Takoda. The eerily comfortable expression she wore made Echo's skin crawl now more than ever. It reminded her of a snake, slithering through grass effortlessly until it lunged for the attack. As Echo had predicted, the girl didn't answer. Ringwaldr sighed but Echo's mind was racing. Why wasn't he being more aggressive? He seemed daft. There had to be more. The noise of the storm had picked up, and Echo felt the thunder rumble through her bones.

"Why aren't you doing more? Don't you think I asked her all this calmly? I brought her here under your orders, and you seem like you aren't trying to get any answers out of her!" Echo shouted. "I know it wasn't in the same language, but do you think asking her anything nicely will work? What did I bring her back for if you're going to have a polite conversation?" After three long days in the forest with all of this mess going on, she had finally had it. Not knowing what to expect when she came back, she certainly hadn't expected a simple conversation. It was strange that a seer who she thought had all the answers, had to question someone he'd already seen in a vision. Everything he had asked Echo to do seemed so vague and out of place, so incoherent and unfulfilling. With all this going on around her, it had finally set her off. All the things she kept bottled up were spilling over and coming out at the worse time.

"Echo, please. Calm down," Takoda said firmly. Her mother had a tone about her that was very kind but condescending at the same time. It drove Echo mad at times.

Ringwaldr cleared his throat and then turned to Asmund who was staring at the stranger as if he were trying to recall where he had seen her before. Asmund was completely caught off guard when Ringwaldr went to whisper something in his ear. Echo already had a feeling of what he'd said when her father turned to her and nodded towards the door. Instead of biting back, Echo angrily walked out and slammed the door behind her. If they were going to leave her out of that mess, she wasn't going to argue even though they were the ones who had gotten her into this mess in the first place.

6
THE POISON

A heavy sigh left Asmund as Echo slammed the door shut behind her. There was a pain in his heart that shone through his eyes, but he had learned how to mask that quickly with his many years in leadership. He knew he was putting his daughter through too much too fast, but this was the life they had. There was no way to change it. No way to turn his back on his people. Not even for his daughter. Asmund gulped down and turned back to Ringwaldr then nodded for him to continue.

"I am inclined to use a different method with the girl, but it will make me vulnerable. I'll need you both to watch her carefully."

Takoda and Asmund exchanged a look, and Asmund nodded to Ringwaldr. Ringwaldr and Takoda switched places. Now Ringwaldr sat across from the girl and Takoda stood behind him.

"Unbind her hands," Ringwaldr demanded. As Asmund did so, he was ready for her to pounce or run. The girl simply smirked and put her hands into Ringwaldr's as he held his out to take hers. Ringwaldr stared into her blue eyes until his own eyes rolled back into his head. Caught in a trance, his back slammed against the chair he was sitting in, and he convulsed. Takoda looked startled as she watched him. The longer he stayed in his convulsion, the blacker the whites of his eyes turned. It made her grimace.

Instantly his eyes shot open and he stood up from his chair, letting go of her hands and turning away from her for a moment.

"Your daughter. She's exhibiting an ability." Confused, Asmund looked from the stranger to Ringwaldr. How he had come to see such a vision from this woman was difficult for him to understand. Takoda immediately went wide-eyed at his words.

"What? What is she exhibiting?" Asmund asked with urgency. Ringwaldr shook his head in confusion.

"I honestly couldn't tell you right now. It's strange." Ringwaldr turned to the redhead at the table and immediately grabbed her by the wrist.

"I read nothing from her. We need to keep her in a cell for now. Maybe she'll talk after a day without food," he snarled, and pulled her up from the chair. As they walked outside the steady downpour fell upon them. The girl surprisingly didn't fight back and kept the same uncomfortable smirk on her face. Ringwaldr ended up dragging her to the soldier's stronghold which wasn't very far.

"Hull, Nejak, make sure this woman doesn't leave your sight. As of right now I will say she is a threat. She refuses to talk and was caught following our scouting group. Keep her here with no food or water until further notice." The two nodded at Ringwaldr's demands and put her in a cell. Then Ringwaldr was off to find Echo. All the while Echo's parents were trailing along, not far behind.

After a short while of sitting on the porch, waiting for the rain to die down, Echo got tired of waiting for nothing. It's not like she could hear anything going on. They were all mumbling in a low tone, and the rain was heavy enough that there wasn't a moment of silence. In her frustration, she decided to check on Kaapo, but when she didn't find him in his cabin, she was a little concerned. She tried the next possibility that she hoped wouldn't be right.

It was easy enough to find him when she entered Eira's cabin because there he was on the bed furthest from the door, surrounded by animal hides and several crystals Eira kept. Echo's eyes widened. Kaapo looked sickly. His brow was drenched with sweat and he was swaying as he sat upright on the bed. Rushing over to his side, her eyes scanned his body. The wound had healed, but it seemed bigger.

"Eira what happened?" Echo looked back to the old

woman who was now standing just behind her looking over Echo's shoulder. The woman heaved a large sigh and shook her head.

"Hello to you too," Kaapo said warily.

"I told him not to shift while he was healing and he never listens to me." With a sad stubborn look Eira took a towel from a wooden bowl beside the bed Kaapo lay in and began to wipe his forehead and neck with it. When she finished she tossed the cloth back in the bowl. Kaapo let out a small cough and thanked her, and then he turned to Echo.

"Glad to see you didn't die."

"Wish I could say the same to you. You look like you're about to at any moment brother. Why did you shift?"

"When I heard the three women had been kidnapped I thought I could help them search the forest."

"Why? Weren't you still healing?"

"That's what I said," Eira chimed in, but Kaapo ignored her.

"It had healed, it wasn't bleeding, I had to change into a mountain lion, a pack almost attacked Piato."

"You should've just—"

"Echo don't tell me what I should and shouldn't do, I understand I shouldn't have changed but I needed to at the time. Please, I've heard enough nagging from mother for the past two days. I don't need it from you too." Echo immediately stopped talking and looked hurt. Kaapo sighed and rubbed his temples with both hands, instantly regretting how temperamental he was with his sister.

"I'm starting to hear things. Smell and taste things differently. I think I can pick up scents."

"Yes, and I told you sickness can bring on delusion," Eira shot at him. "Your brother thinks his abilities are getting stronger, and I think if he's right, let's just hope he can heal and control them, because I've never seen a shifter this ill before. I just broke two fevers in two days. If you have another, I don't know if you'll still be sane through it!" Eira finished and pushed Kaapo down gently by his shoulders so that he would lie down. The boy didn't struggle, welcoming the gesture, because when he lay back, he seemed relieved.

Both Eira and Echo turned to the door when they heard a loud knock. Ringwaldr pushed his way in and looked to Echo.

"Echo, we need to talk," he demanded, and Echo scoffed.

"You just kicked me out and now you want me to listen to you?"

"Now," he snarled, and this time Echo wanted to bite back, opening her mouth to cuss him out, but when she saw her parents follow in behind him she closed it because she couldn't understand the startled look on their faces.

"Echo what happened during the scouting? Did you use an ability? What was it darling?" her mother asked very gently, coming over to her and wrapping an arm around her. Kaapo sat upright in his bed, surprised

114

about what he had heard. Eira attempted to push him back down again but this time he stopped her so he could stay sitting.

"Why didn't you tell us the moment you got home?" Her father asked, and Echo didn't know how to answer all these questions at once. Her mother was trying to walk her out of Eira's but Echo stood firmly in the middle of the cabin to collect her bearings. All Echo wanted her whole life was to have an ability, and all at once she wished that she had been more careful of what she had wished for.

"I didn't- I don't even know what I did! It didn't feel real, I can't remember what happened, I thought it was more important to tell you I caught a wildly odd stranger. I come back to find my brother is falling apart, and we don't know whether or not an attack is coming because the scouting went so horribly! Maybe it's just me, but I didn't feel like telling everyone about something I don't even understand is happening to me!" As Echo explained everything in her incoherent ramblings, she finally felt a giant weight leave her shoulders. Even when she knew she had all this responsibility still, it was nice to finally scream out all her frustration.

Takoda pulled Echo into a hug, holding her with a sense of security. It comforted Echo, but not in a way that would last because when her mother let go of her she still had to deal with everyone staring at her.

"I think... for now... we all need a bit of rest, especially my children. We can speak about this tomorrow morning." Takoda pushed some hair away from Echo's face and tucked it behind her daughter's ear, then pushed past Ringwaldr and her husband at the door to lead Echo out. In silence they walked back to Echo's cabin, while Takoda still held Echo tightly at her side. Echo felt like a disappointment, like maybe she was in trouble for saying all of that and getting angry so quickly. Even though her mother had just pulled her out of a tight spot, she still felt like she was in trouble for not meeting a standard. When they got to Echo's cabin, Takoda sat down with her on her bed.

"You need some rest. I can tell you haven't slept well, and don't worry about the scouting. We sent a second group out to look for our stolen women. They will alert us if need be," Takoda explained calmly, and Echo sighed. It was a little bit of a relief, but it only made Echo feel like more of a failure.

"I wanted to tell you Echo… no matter what," Takoda took some of Echo's hair in her hands and began to braid it. The gesture made Echo grin sadly. Her mother hadn't done her hair since she was a small girl. "I am so proud of you. I wish that I could show you more. I realize that your father and I have been distant lately, but it's only because you and Kaapo are not our only children. This entire tribe are our sons and daughters, our mothers and fathers, our brothers and sisters, and right now, I need to make sure that I keep *all* of you safe. I'm so worried for the women taken. I hoped there was another way…" Takoda took a deep breath and closed her eyes as she breathed out.

Echo suddenly felt like her mother realized what Echo was feeling because she was feeling the same thing: a kind of pressure to uphold a certain standard. Whether someone set that standard for her or she had set it for herself.

It was a bit of a relief to know her mighty mother felt just as overwhelmed as Echo sometimes. Echo had no reply, her mother was right, Echo was exhausted, and she was thankful her mother had taken her out of another tiring situation. She was still looking out for Echo even when she had been stretched so thin. The two exchanged a short goodbye when Echo didn't know what else to say, and Echo lay in bed until she soon passed out.

Restless and exasperated Echo kept fidgeting in her bed. With how unstill she was it was as if her bed was a boat on rocky waters. After she had passed out, it may have been roughly three or four hours later that she was tousling back and forth again. When she finally couldn't take it anymore she sat upright.

Tap, tap... tap, tap.

Startled, Echo's stomach turned. It sounded like a knock on her door, but she didn't think anyone would be up at this hour. Fighting all her exhausted instincts to go back to sleep, she stood from her bed and slowly walked over to her door.

Not being one for tension Echo quickly opened it

and let it swing freely.

No one.

Echo thought and walked out of her door to make certain. The torches that lit the pathway to the other cabins were as bright as they were when they were first lit in the evening and she wondered for a moment why there was a sort of green haze around a few of them.

I must be dreaming...

Biting her lip, Echo felt a pull in the pit of her stomach. Even with how uncomfortable the situation was making her she listened to her instincts to follow the green haze down the path. The green glowing haze seemed to get stronger the closer Echo got to... *Eira's cabin?*

When Echo noticed Eira's door was wide open she sprinted to it, only then realizing when she got to the doorway that she hadn't taken any sort of weapon with her had there been a reason to use one. Then she remembered the knife still strapped to her calf.

"You'll need this for later little mouse."

An unfamiliar voice whispered in the dark, and Echo's eyes suddenly adjusted to notice something very telling of the stranger standing beside Kaapo's bed. There was one candle lit on Eira's table that made the stranger's red hair glisten. It was the girl. The redheaded monster. She was holding Kaapo's arm and whispering nonsense in the dark. Echo couldn't see what she was doing clearly, so she grabbed a torch from the wall beside the door and set it over the flame of the candle on the table. When the flame caught, the whole cabin was flooded with light.

There, Echo witnessed the young girl holding Kaapo's arm as a black smoke engulfed it. It seemed to come from her hands. The black smoke became embedded in Kaapo's skin and caused strange boils upon it.

"Get away from him!" Echo screamed and thrust the torch towards her. In a panic, the girl let go of Kaapo's arm and ran off, but not before an eerily familiar laugh escaped her. She ran off into the night. Echo gaped as the girl ran past the path lit by torches and into the cover of darkness before she turned back to her brother.

"Kaapo! Kaapo wake up!" Echo pleaded at his side and the boy suddenly stirred. When he awoke the boils on his skin began to boil up and pop, disappearing as they did but the dark colour lingered. He took one look at his arm and jumped.

"What did you do!" he asked in a frightened whisper.

"It wasn't me!" Echo answered and took his blackened hand in one of hers. "Does it hurt?"

"No… but why is it like that?" Kaapo asked wide-eyed. The black colour that overtook his skin finally dissipated. His regular tanned skin tone came back to life, and both of the siblings exchanged frightened looks.

"The stranger was in here. She said something about a mouse? She's probably run off into the forest now, and I really don't feel like chasing that lunatic in the dark for the second time." Kaapo was barely listening to Echo as he had no idea of what she meant. He sat upright looking over his hand again and again, running his opposite hand over it to make sure it was still fully intact.

"What in a bloody red moon was all that screaming about?" It seems their encounter had awakened Eira who had been in another bed in a smaller room of the cabin. From the way her hair stood up in several directions on her head told the siblings that she awoke rather abruptly.

"Eira look at Kaapo's...arm..." Echo slowly realized maybe his arm was okay because the black substance she had seen seemed to subside.

"What is it?" The old woman groaned and grabbed Kaapo's arm a little too hard yanking him just a tad closer to the bed's edge.

"I don't see anything. I know I'm practically blind but what am I supposed to be looking for?" Frustrated, she gave his arm back to him.

"It was like a black smoke, and there were boils I swear!" Kaapo answered.

"Black boils?" Eira gasped as her eyes became wide, "Did it settle!" Eira was moving quicker now, rummaging through her worktable for something in particular. When she found it, she made a quick movement towards Kaapo and the back of his hand was sliced open in an instant. Echo shrieked and knocked the knife out of Eira's hand but when she looked back at Kaapo she was completely stunned.

A black smoke oozed its way out of the cut and instead of disappearing it took the shape of a small creature that had the feathery wings of a bird but the head of a mouse. It jumped from Kaapo's hand, who had been screaming the entire time, and flew around before Eira chased after it with her broom shooing it out of her cabin completely. When the door closed everyone went silent and didn't know where to look first. Kaapo looked to his hand and shuddered. There was no blood, not even a gash. He didn't feel strong enough to stand but he couldn't sit either. He suddenly became incredibly agitated.

"What was that!" he shouted towards Eira. The old woman came to his side and looked at his hand.

"Whole? No blood… that's odd," Eira mumbled to herself.

"Please Eira, just explain," Echo whined. The old woman looked to her and then her brother. She had questions of her own but for now she'd relieve them with some answers.

"It was a black Harmak. Filthy things, ridden with a poison. Their counterpart, the red Harmak have the antidote, if you don't cut it out of you fast enough… you'll need it. I'm concerned. I cut it out but usually it's just the smoke, not the entire bloody bird, and there was no blood. There has to be blood or it could mean there's still something in there. I've never seen someone not bleed after doing that."

"Why do things keep attacking me!" Kaapo shouted.

Echo didn't want to sound like a know-it-all when her brother was clearly having a very bad time but technically, he had gotten himself in the past two situations. This one was kind of unfair. There was no reason for that girl to attack him. She didn't even know Kaapo. Why was she picking on the already sick and injured?

"Echo go get your parents. Bring them here. I don't want to jump to conclusions, but we may need a bowman to go out and hunt down a red Harmak. I don't want to take any chances your brother is already weak enough."

Echo nodded in response and took off for her parent's cabin but not before she saw Kaapo angrily lie back down in his bed. She wondered why he was taking the brunt of everything. Both situations now had started with a choice Echo had made indirectly. Echo wanted to go hunting knowing full well her brother wouldn't listen to her and stay away. Echo brought that strange girl back only to have her do this. It seemed like a very bad pattern that she wanted to break.

7
THE HUNT

There was a collective silence throughout the massive soldiers' stronghold. A steady wind came through the windows, causing the many colourful tapestries on the walls to flutter and stir. Once Echo had relayed the information of the attack on her brother to her parents, they gathered the Hemeran elders, and whatever soldiers they could wake before dawn. Asmund stood at the head of a long table that seated twenty-four men and women of his tribe and took a deep breath.

"It has come to my attention that Iivona may have a secret that I never thought would be possible. In all my years of experience with this tribe, they have kept their distance from us and our abilities, calling us the tribe of demons born of demon waters." The room stayed quiet as Asmund struggled to continue. His stature never changed but his pauses told everyone that this was difficult for him to discuss.

"The stranger we had held captive has escaped, and before doing so she has poisoned my son with a black Harmak with an ability my daughter witnessed, and that no one has ever seen before. I will need several fire bringers to send up an emergency signal to the group of men I sent to the wall to find our taken women. They need to be called back. Now that we don't know entirely what we are dealing with, I'd like them home before we lose anymore. Awal, Lyn, please." Asmund nodded to a man and woman at the end of the table. Two very skilled fire bringers of the tribe who knew how to send up a signal like a flare. The two got up in an instant and walked outside of the stronghold. It was early morning, so the light of the sunrise entered the candlelit room.

"We have sent messengers, but it seems that they are not responding. They leave a message at the wall and are not let in. Ringwaldr has let me know that his visions only ever show us attacking first, and if there is any change to that, he will let us know. So I am telling everyone now... to ready yourselves." Asmund finished and nodded to the door. Everyone in the room took that as a signal to leave.

In the corner of the room, Echo was leaning against the wall beside her mother. She was still having trouble with what had happened the previous night. She had told her parents everything she saw. Except she neglected to tell them about the green haze that led her there. She didn't know how to explain that part.

"Echo, I'll need you to get Hanuel and Manson on that Harmak," Asmund demanded. Echo slowly got up from her leaning position and walked to the door. Before she left she turned back to her father.

She wanted to ask him questions. She had a dark feeling in the pit of her stomach about Iivona. Her father was always the type of man to be short and concise, but when it came to Iivona, she could tell he knew more, he just didn't know how to explain. Or maybe he just didn't want to. Fighting the urge to question him knowing that time was of the essence, she headed out the door and off to Hanuel's family cabin.

As she ran down the path she noticed a few hunters going towards the forest with spears and bows. Quickly she scanned them making sure that none of them were Manson, knowing he sometimes went out with the gatherers to help get food for their tribe. Once she got to Hanuel's she knocked softly on his door. Her breathing sped up suddenly, remembering that the last time Hanuel and her had really spoken it was after their-

"Echo, why so early?" Hanuel's mother Xerxa asked. Xerxa gave none of her looks to her son, only her curls. She had a much more feminine face that was certainly different from Hanuel's sharper features.

"Sorry, I'm here for Hanuel, my father's orders. We need him to help catch a Harmak. It's urgent," Echo said softly, and Xerxa smiled and pulled Echo in by the shoulder gently.

"He's still asleep as expected, wake him if you wish."

Xerxa grinned and went over to a tall cabinet at the opposite side of the cabin. Echo noticed she caught the woman getting ready for the day as Xerxa was pulling out her farming tools. Echo looked over to the back room nervously. It wasn't the first time she had to wake Hanuel but it was the first time she was anxious about it. She took a deep breath and shook this ridiculous feeling off. It was just Hanuel and she had a job to do. Time was of the essence.

"Wake up!" Echo said a little loudly, pushing Hanuel's door open abruptly to let it swing and clank. She could see the boy stir and furrow his eyebrows as his face was half in his cot and half faced towards the door. Xerxa let out a small laugh.

"Wake up!" She repeated and walked over to lightly slap his cheek a couple of times. Hanuel was shocked by the sudden movement and went wide-eyed. When he noticed it was just Echo he yawned and grinned mischievously.

"I'll only wake if you use gentler tactics." Echo rolled her eyes at him.

"Do you even know who I am?" Echo grabbed his arm and pulled him so he was sitting up. "Come on we have to catch a bird."

"I don't want a bloody bird for breakfast. Catch it yourself."

"It's not for breakfast genius, it's for my brother. He was poisoned last night by that stranger and now we have to get Manson and go hunt a Harmak." Hanuel opened his eyes wide and slapped both of his cheeks with his hands. Echo stood in front of him with her arms crossed over her chest as she tapped her foot impatiently.

"Sounds like I missed a lot, and a Harmak? You mean those dumb flying things we're always trying to avoid on hunts? Those things hurt my ears," Hanuel complained and got to his feet.

"I'm sorry, but you're the only scout who can hear them from miles away, so let's get going."

Hanuel sighed and scratched the back of his head before standing, which made his wild curls stand up as well. Echo's throat went dry at the sudden thought of running her hand through his hair, and she shook the thought out of her head immediately.

Quickly, she left his room so he could change. Before going out to the porch to wait, she waved goodbye to his mother who had left for the day. Shortly after, Hanuel came out in his usual buckskins with his satchel across his body. Hanuel flashed Echo a smile when he emerged from the door, noticing that she seemed lost in her thoughts.

"Your hair is stuck."

"Huh?" Mindlessly Echo touched her hair but didn't really fix whatever problem Hanuel was seeing. Gently he lifted her satchel strap just an inch off her shoulder and unwound her hair that had been stuck to it. Echo thought of all the other times he had done that for her and wondered if maybe he felt what she had been feeling now for much longer than she had. All the times he had done little things like grab her hand to show her something, or help make her feel better, or fix her hair. Did he have the same yearning feeling in his heart and stomach? Or was he just doing those things without thinking? They were so used to each other after years of spending everyday together. Again, she was easily lost in her thoughts and only noticed that Hanuel had walked a little bit down the path before shaking herself out of her trance and following behind him. The two were on their way to Manson's cabin which was only a short distance away.

"Get your bow, we're hunting Harmak!" Hanuel yelled at the top of his lungs and beat on the door several times after Echo had already knocked politely at Manson's family door.

"You have the grace of a rockslide, Hanuel."

Hanuel shrugged off Echo's comment but didn't disagree, and gave Manson a pat on the back as he came out, readily dressed. The three started walking off the porch and down the path.

"That was quick," Echo remarked in disbelief.

"Yeah well, my father told me what happened in the meeting at sunrise and I figured I'd get a head start."

"Wait there was a meeting at sunrise about this?" Hanuel asked.

"Echo didn't tell you?" Manson smirked.

"Echo doesn't tell me anything she just yells at me to do something and I blindly follow." That managed to get Hanuel a deathly glare and a scoff from the girl as the three made their way down the path to the forest. Echo swatted at his shoulder playfully but he dodged and she missed. "I didn't mean it as a bad thing! I'll follow you anywhere Echo. Even up a tree I can't climb."

Echo's glare turned into a grin and her cheeks went red when Manson smirked over at her. To hide her embarrassment, she rummaged through her satchel to find and break some pemmican for the three of them to share and eat before they were swallowed by the large trees and flora of the forest.

They walked along for several minutes then broke into a jog once Hanuel had caught the sound of the chirping creature. Echo wished they could have Jillik use his ability on this outing but the boy only sensed things in the ground. From what Echo knew of the Harmak they were always in the air or trees or even caves. Even though everything is connected, Jillik could really only sense something that came in contact with the dirt. He was helpful at sensing footsteps but not airborne creatures.

"I just saw one! These things are so irritating. If they flew in flocks they'd be easier to aim at," said Manson after flinging his arrow into the air with no success.

"You have to watch where you're aiming. Don't get it in the head. Remember what I told you. Eira said it's best if it's not dead," Echo warned him. Manson reached for another arrow from his quiver to aim out to the trees but sighed when he noticed he'd lost sight of it completely.

"Can you hear where it's going?" Manson asked Hanuel.

"No, it's not chirping, and I can't tell the difference

between its wings and regular birds' wings if I'm being honest. If it was in that direction, I can guess it's further that way, but it's probably landed in a tree," Hanuel responded. The three walked a little further in the direction Hanuel pointed in.

The group was on their way again, and hadn't noticed how much time had gone by until Echo looked up at the afternoon sun glistening through the trees. At the very least, there was no storm like there had been the other day. That much she was grateful for, but the time it was taking to find this evasive creature made her fear for her brother's life. Eira hadn't said how long they had to help Kaapo but she said as soon as humanly possible. She also said once injured, the bird could live for a while, but if the edges of the bird's wings turned black, they couldn't use it. Meaning they had to get back fast with the bird once hit with an arrow, which she had hoped would be easy enough with Manson's speed.

"Hanuel what's the chirping sound like? Can we try to call it?" Echo finally asked him as they were walking and he shrugged.

"I can try. It's like a high-pitched stutter. Happens in threes," Hanuel said before trying to replicate it. It seemed like he didn't get it when Manson laughed at the attempt.

"That sounds nothing like it."

"Then you try genius," Hanuel said. Manson opened his mouth to try but Echo beat him to it. She figured the boys wouldn't have the range because their voices were too deep. The first attempt from Echo sounded pretty close, but when they all paused for a response there was nothing. Manson nodded to her in approval to do it again and Echo proceeded. The second time there was a stir in the trees, and the three of them caught a glimpse of red. All of them froze in place. Unsure of what movements would startle the bird, Echo chirped one last time.

The small red creature came into the brush of trees with them. It unsuspectingly sat atop a branch fairly close and Manson aimed his bow. Getting a better look at it, the creature had the head of a mouse and long stringy ears that sat upright. The rest of its body looked like a glistening red cardinal. Echo kept her eyes on it without blinking. She could feel a very large pull in her heart. Everything rode on Manson making that shot. The young man was about to let an arrow soar when the bird changed directions and made a very large swoop to get away. As it flew past Echo she felt a sinking feeling in her stomach.

You're not getting away.

She was right. The bird had no chance to get away. Echo blinked her eyes and was suddenly holding the bird tightly in both of her hands. Breathing heavily, she looked back at the two young men who were frozen in place, staring wide-eyed at her.

"What happened?" Echo asked slowly, not even sure if she wanted to know the answer. Whenever she blinked and didn't remember something, she knew it was quickly followed by a green haze behind her. There it was, the green haze, and the sinking feeling in her stomach that followed. What was she doing? Better yet, why was her leg in so much pain?

"Echo!" Hanuel shouted and she looked down at where he was looking. A giant gash graced her left thigh, oozing an amount of blood that Echo had never seen leave her own body. She stumbled, trying to keep both hands on the wiggling bird, and stay standing. Hanuel and Manson ran over. Manson snatched the bird from her hands and tucked its head under its wing to try to put it to sleep. Hanuel grabbed Echo and sat her down slowly as she was already heading for the ground.

Without hesitation he ripped through his satchel for some spare material to tie around her leg.

"Echo, I'm gonna tie this. It's gonna hurt. Manson will run you to Eira's as fast as possible." Echo nodded her head in wide-eyed shock as reality sunk in around her. She was quickly putting together the pieces in her head. Echo lunged for the bird, Manson shot an arrow at the same time, and it sliced open the side of her thigh. Although in shock she was thankful it didn't get her in the head. Hanuel finished tying up her leg, and Manson tossed him the bird he'd put to sleep. Then Manson easily swiped up Echo, cradling her in his arms and took off at an alarming rate.

All was quiet at the Hemera settlement until Manson came barging out of the forest with Echo in his arms.

With the blood-soaked rag around her leg, and the simple fact that she was the leader's daughter, it was a shocking sight to see her being taken to the healer's cabin in such a way. By the time Manson got to the edge of the forest he was so tired, he had returned to his regular jogging speed. Thankfully he managed to make it to Eira's cabin before Echo passed out from the sheer shock.

"What happened my boy?" Eira asked as he gently lay Echo down on the bed next to Kaapo's. By this time Echo was writhing in pain, her teeth were clenched and she couldn't stop thinking about her burning wound.

"I nicked her with my arrow."

"Manson I'll kill you!" Kaapo shouted from his bed, but he was shushed by Eira and stayed in place.

"It was an accident Kaapo, don't be daft! She moved when she wasn't supposed to!" Manson shot back.

"Quiet down both of you. Manson I'm aware you use dry higara on your arrowheads? Sleeping rash root?" Eira said calmly and went over to the table to grab astringent. Manson nodded, looking slightly ashamed but Eira seemed to be unbothered, where Echo seemed more frightened at the answer. Without warning Eira snipped off the makeshift bandage on Echo's leg and doused it in the homemade concoction. Echo seethed like her brother had the first time. Now she really knew how that stuff felt when there was a lot of it in a wound. Eira nodded to Manson to grab her several things from around the room, one of them being a very strange looking metal instrument and a bowl.

"Wait, what're you doing?" Echo asked fearfully, and Eira didn't answer.

"Manson you're gonna have to hold your friend down. I know she can be known to flail," Eira said. Echo looked wide-eyed over at Manson.

"Manson you hold me down and *I'll* kill you!"

"Both of you are terrible to me, why am I even friends with you two?" Manson rolled his eyes and tried to grab a hold of Echo's arms but she took to swatting at his head fiercely and he had to hold up his arms to protect himself.

"Echo!" Eira shouted and Echo's swatting immediately stopped. "Drink some of this. It'll calm your nerves and ensure that herb won't make you too drowsy and itchy. It's a miracle you haven't felt any of those symptoms yet. The wound has pieces of debris in it. I need to get them out or you'll fall ill with a terrible fever. Let us help you," Eira said in her usual tough love tone. Echo frowned, still a little wild-eyed, and heaved a wincing sigh. Noticing how tired and out of breath Manson was from running her all the way here she realized she was being a spoiled brat. She had to toughen up, and when she saw Hanuel burst through the door a little bit of relief went through her.

"Fine," she responded meekly and took a giant swig of the bottled astringent. The smell and taste were horrible and she gagged after drinking just a little bit, but Hanuel rushed to her side, and she held onto his and Manson's hand as Eira began to pick pieces of stone out of the wound. Manson was known to use very jagged arrow heads that could break on contact with anything so there were pieces of the arrowhead as well as debris from the forest floor stuck in her wound.

"Did you at least find the bird?" Eira asked as she began slowly moving the metal picking tool into Echo's gash. The girl winced and tried her hardest not to cry out in pain but still a cry escaped her. Hanuel gently pushed Echo's hair behind her ear and squeezed her shoulder reassuringly. Then he reached into his bag and gingerly pulled out the bird.

"I'm surprised it didn't wake up while I ran here," he said in disbelief and brought it over to Kaapo.

"Eat it. Like that," Eira said shortly as she took the bottle astringent from Echo's hand and doused her leg in it. The girl cried out in pain, louder this time.

Kaapo and Hanuel shared a confused look and Hanuel handed Kaapo the bird.

"Good luck with that friend." Hanuel patted Kaapo on the shoulder and headed back over to Echo who had her eyes closed hard now, trying not to watch as Eira pulled more bits out of her leg.

"I'm going to go get your parents," Hanuel said urgently to her as he gently pushed her hair back behind her ear again to kiss her on the cheek, then he took off through the front door.

"Well, that was cute," Manson smirked, and Echo squeezed his hand hard enough for him to curse. From the look in Echo's eyes, Manson could tell it was the wrong time for teasing.

Looking from the bird to the back of the old

woman's head confusedly Kaapo sighed and rolled his eyes. Slamming his eyes shut and bracing for the impact of moving wings, Kaapo shoved the bird's head into his mouth. He grimaced as he bit down and heard a crunch. Instead of uncontrollable flapping of wings he felt the bird suddenly lose mass and turn into smoke in his hands. Even though it moved like smoke, it felt solid going down his throat. He couldn't breathe. When he finally choked down the solid he had felt, he wiped at his mouth, thinking something would be there but there was nothing. No feathers. Not even blood. Instantly he felt like a new man, even after the disgusting act of chewing off a bird's head whole. It was a strange feeling. The feeling of smoke ran through him and made his body feel light and relaxed, rather than heavy with sickness like it had been before. He looked over at his writhing sister who looked like she was so angry she could beat the life out of Eira.

"Remember Echo never hit an elder, also she knows what she's talking about so hang in there." His encouraging words seemed to frustrate her even more but she didn't have the energy to talk back. All she could think about was the pain of her open gash and the ever so constant pain of a cold metal tool poking at it making it burn. It wasn't long before Eira was finished prodding Echo with a poker, and was now beginning to stitch her. After two small skilful pricks she was finally finished and the constant pain that plagued Echo eased up just a little. She closed her eyes and laid back. Manson put a cold cloth of water on her head as Eira had instructed him and she thanked him before everyone in the room was startled by the front door swinging open abruptly.

8
THE FALL ON DEAF EARS

In the dimly lit soldiers' cabin at the large table sat Asmund and Ringwaldr facing each other. They looked a little ridiculous taking up only two seats of the twenty-four at the very end of it Takoda paced back and forth beside it as if she had nowhere to sit. With a racing mind, the mere notion of sitting didn't exist to her.

"How many times do I have to argue with you on this, Asmund. Ringwaldr has sent several messengers now and none of them are coming back with good news. Iivona is not looking for a resolution and I fear they will strike when we are not fully prepared." Finally, Takoda stopped moving back and forth beside the two and put her fist down on the table. Asmund looked at her and sighed deeply.

"I realize this, but Ringwaldr has not seen an attack

initiated by them. I don't want us to look like the brutes! How many times must I say it, if we show up with an army it will seem like an attack," he retaliated.

"Is that really what you're afraid of them thinking Asmund? Or are you scared of what someone else thinks?" There was venom in those words. Asmund could hear it in her tone. Choosing to stay silent he stood from his seat and walked over to the nearest window to stare out at the dirt pathway. There were few people around. It was the afternoon. Most of his people were tending to their daily tasks.

"We'll make sure everyone is on guard, but we will not be the first to attack. That isn't who we are Takoda, and your anger is getting the best of you." Asmund met Takoda's gaze as he turned around, and felt her piercing, green eyes burning holes in his skin. He knew she'd be unhappy with him, but Ringwaldr and everything in his gut told him not to attack.

"There is a difference between us attacking them, and us merely going to them fully prepared, rather than waiting around like sitting ducks Asmund. It's almost as if you're not hearing me!" Without warning Takoda headed for the door, swinging it open and slamming it shut as she left. It seems she was done trying to talk sense into him. It was in Hemera's best interest to not go to Iivona with an army. The Hemeran soldiers were made up of mostly strongmen like Asmund himself. Few fire bringers, and two other men who had an ability that could down a man in an instant if used correctly. It was something unexplainable to his people but said ability could send a man into convulsions until he hit the ground. Nevertheless, as Asmund had said so many times before, *it could incite violence to show up with an army, especially an army so deadly without human-made weapons.*

He had said that over and over again to Takoda. She was still insistent that they go ready and willing to fight but not with that plan in mind. The two just could not see eye to eye, but even in the worst of disagreements they could stay together. At this time, Asmund felt their relationship was hindering. Recently, he had told Takoda about something of his past with Iivona and it had made her distant with him.

Ringwaldr sat in silence as he watched the two bicker. Now that he felt it was safe to finally speak, without the wrath of Takoda on him, he stood.

"This may be a bad time to bring this up, but we need to ensure that your daughter is coming into her abilities properly. It's important that she works on her skill."

"I agree, but what have you seen of Kaapo? My boy seems to get more ill with every passing day."

"It will pass sooner than you think. He is of little concern right now." Asmund seemed offended when Ringwaldr said that and was about to ask him why he was so unbothered by Kaapo's illness when he spotted Hanuel through the corner of his eye running to the cabin. Asmund opened the door mid-knock.

"Hanuel?"

"Is Takoda with you? Echo is at Eira's. She was

wounded in the forest." Asmund's heart sank but he began to walk out of the room grabbing Hanuel's arm and dragging him. Ringwaldr followed quickly behind them both.

"Ringwaldr you didn't see this?"

"No, there was no injury to your daughter in my visions."

"She was grazed by an arrow," Hanuel said as he looked to Ringwaldr, a little in disbelief that he hadn't seen anything.

Asmund seemed furious suddenly. He wasn't mentally prepared for another injured child right now.

"Why wouldn't you have seen this? I specifically asked you to focus on her."

"I've been focusing on a lot of things lately, Asmund. There are a lot of paths. I must follow the ones that are the most likely and dire." Asmund shook his head and barged through Eira's door.

Startled, everyone in the room jumped at the sound. Eira shushed him angrily.

"I don't care who you think you are Asmund! You don't go breaking down my door with that immense power of yours!" she snarled. Asmund seemed to forcefully calm himself at the words, knowing Eira wasn't above swatting him with a broom as she had when he was a child being unruly. "Your daughter is fine. She is in my care after all."

"What happened?" He looked from Hanuel to Kaapo then to Echo on the bed who was now staring at him wide-eyed. Seeing as the siblings were startled and Manson was too afraid to speak; Hanuel spoke up for him.

"We were hunting the Harmak and she... well the thing was in a tree and then it swooped down and Manson had aimed for it. It was a bit away from Echo but she somehow caught it, and the arrow that Manson let fly grazed her leg." Trying to explain with actions, Hanuel ended up looking like a man trying to dance and not quite getting the rhythm down as he swung his arms about. Asmund moved closer to Manson with a dreaded look in his eye and Echo held her arm up to stop him.

"Wait a minute," she seethed in pain. "It was a complete accident. I jumped in front of it. He wasn't aiming for me, father." Disregarding what she said Asmund still grabbed Manson by his leather chest plate.

"She caught the bird in her bare hands?" Asmund asked as he looked down at Manson. The boy was too nervous and shocked to answer. Hanuel rushed to speak again.

"Yes, and she wasn't anywhere near it before that. Also someone is calling your name very loudly, Asmund," Hanuel explained to Asmund.

Looking deeply into Manson's eyes with a brooding expression Asmund let the boy go from his grip and suddenly heard what Hanuel was talking about but at a lower volume. Manson looked deathly pale from fright and backed up as much as he could from Asmund to stand in the corner. Echo mouthed the word 'sorry' to him.

"What in the world could need my attention now?" he breathed, rubbing his temples in frustration. Asmund walked over and swung the front door open, which made Eira scoff at him.

"I'm here," he shouted back. The man who had been calling his name ran over. He was out of breath.

"The captured women, they were brought back! They're at the pit." The man hunched over clutching his knees as he breathlessly got the words out.

"All were rescued?" Asmund asked.

"All," the man confirmed.

"I'll be right there," Asmund answered and then turned to Hanuel. "Tell her mother. But… Manson should leave now before Takoda shows up. Her wrath is much harder to contain than mine." Hanuel responded with a curt nod then took off out the door. Asmund nodded to Ringwaldr to follow him out. Before leaving, Asmund made a point to gently close the front door as he flashed Eira a pointed look. Manson gulped down and gave Echo a short hug before fleeing from the cabin.

As Asmund came to the pit, the very large area where the tribe held their nightly bonfires, he rushed to Frea's side to help her off the horse-driven cart. The women kidnapped all had the same bewildered look on their face and similar facial features except Frea who seemed to be about twenty years older than Ver and Avila. Frea had long and wispy grey hair and piercing blue eyes set against dark tanned skin. She was a very skilled water bringer who had never been as tempered as she was now. The change in character startled Asmund.

"Asmund, tell me why we were kidnapped only to be thrown into a dark cave to find our way out!" She jabbed Asmund in the chest with every other word. Her bony little finger disappeared into his very long, dark beard each time. Her small stature compared to his was almost comical. She was a mouse standing up to a lion.

"What? Where did you find them?" Asmund turned to one of the soldiers helping the other ladies down from the cart.

"We could see the wall of Iivona when we noticed the signal you sent up to come back. Then as we were turning back we caught Avila running towards Hemera. She brought us to the cave she had come from. That's where we found Frea and Ver."

"Yes! And I don't even know how she found her way out! It seemed like Ver was the only other voice I could hear in that cave! I was stuck in a vein of it and Ver seemed to be a few steps away but there was a rock wall between us! We only got out because she did!" Frea pointed that same bony finger that was hitting Asmund in the chest at Avila and the girl looked bewildered.

"I had a vision that led me to an opening." Avila swayed, and held her stomach as if she were about to be sick. "My mind has never been so scattered," she let out in shock.

"I'm taking her to get rest," Ringwaldr said shortly and led the girl away to their cabin.

"So you're telling me they were just dropped in a

cave outside Iivona with no guards, nothing?" Asmund said slowly trying to get the story straight.

"It seems that way, friend," the soldier answered, just as confused as Asmund. Ver ran over to her family to be embraced. She didn't seem to be in any state to speak so Asmund didn't want to press the issue.

"Thank you soldiers, for returning our tribe's women to their families. For now, let's be thankful we are a whole tribe again. Everyone get some rest. Don't worry about any responsibilities today and make sure wherever you travel near the edge of the forest you have someone with you," Asmund bellowed and then headed off.

"Hey! Psst!"

The light of a single candle barely lit up the healer's cabin in the dead of night. Kaapo was wide awake out of boredom in his bed and was trying to wake up Hanuel who was out cold in the chair between Kaapo and Echo's beds, with his head resting just beside Echo's arm. When Hanuel didn't stir, Kaapo took to throwing small pieces of rolled up bandages at him. He'd fallen asleep not too long ago. After Takoda came in to help Eira clean Echo's wound she sat with Echo for a while, but Echo had been so exhausted, that the rest of the afternoon went by in a blur. Eira assumed it was from the sleeping rash root. Then she woke up to the smell of stew and ate something. After that, Hanuel, Kaapo, and Echo talked for a little until Hanuel and Echo fell asleep.

Hanuel hadn't left once during the whole night. He wanted to make sure Echo fell asleep before he did, but it seemed even though she was injured she had more stamina than him because she ended up falling asleep just in time for him to pass out as well. Now it was like a sport for Kaapo to try and wake up the boy who could supposedly hear a mouse's footsteps from miles away. Kaapo couldn't believe how difficult it was. Groggily, Hanuel woke up after noticing the weight of rolled up bandages piling up on his head.

"Man, you're hard to wake up for a guy who can hear the entire forest all the time," Kaapo snorted and then sighed. "You should go home friend. Either that or help me get some ink from Eira's pot so I can write something on my sister's forehead while she's still out." Kaapo joked but Hanuel seemed too tired to laugh. Kaapo took a deep breath and shook his head. "If I were an actual fool like everyone thinks I am, I wouldn't notice that you might be here next to my sister because you care a little more than usual."

"Or maybe I just don't want her to find an awful marking on her cheek when she finally wakes." Hanuel shrugged as he pulled all the bandages out of his curls that Kaapo had thrown at him. Kaapo laughed lightly in disbelief that he'd say no to drawing something on Echo. They used to do it all the time when they were kids sleeping by the fire.

"I'm pretty good at drawing Hanuel. I don't know what you're talking about."

"Even your writing is terrible, Kaapo. What do you think you could draw?" Echo said as she yawned. It was hard to stay asleep after hearing her brother laugh. Even when he was trying to be quiet, he was still bad at being quiet. Groaning, Echo shifted herself from side to side until she was sitting up in her bed. Rubbing the sleep out of her eyes she looked over to Hanuel whose big curly head of hair was coming into focus.

"How does it look?" Echo looked down at her thigh and back up at Hanuel.

"It's just a scratch." Hanuel shrugged, and Echo smirked, it sure hadn't felt that way. When she became a little more aware of her surroundings she looked over at her brother.

"So, the bird didn't work? Why are you still here?" Echo asked her brother.

"What, I'm not allowed to show concern for my sister? The darling little Echo?"

"I didn't say that, but you're not the type." Kaapo shook his head, frustrated by her response.

"I know you're sick of seeing me in this bed. Believe me, I'm sick of being here, but Eira said I should stay for another night. She wants to make sure we're both not on death's door after the few days we've had." Echo nodded in understanding, and then looked back to Hanuel, noticing he looked rather tired.

"Is it still night? Did you get any sleep?" Echo asked as she lifted his chin with her hand to take a look at the ever-growing bags underneath his eyes.

"I'm fine. I slept a little."

Kaapo snorted at Hanuel's response.

"The only time he left your side was to get mom, and then when mom left, he sat beside you there like a pet," Kaapo said smugly. Hanuel's eyes shifted around as he was ratted out by Kaapo. "I don't know why you're embarrassed Hanuel. I'd give anything to have a pretty person like you tend to me when I was ill." Completely ignoring Kaapo, Hanuel sighed and looked at Echo.

"Did you need anything?" It felt strange to stare at Hanuel's lips and want to answer him with a kiss but she realized that's something she probably shouldn't be doing in front of her brother, or his perpetual teasing would get worse. She gulped down and nodded yes.

"Is there any stew left?" Echo asked, her eyes lighting up with hope. For a moment Hanuel looked like he was going to disappoint her by saying no but he smirked in that way of his and nodded before getting up to go get her some from a pot on a far table.

"Guess you're not gonna get me any huh, friend?" Kaapo smirked and Hanuel scoffed and rolled his eyes at him.

"You can walk just fine. Get it yourself," Hanuel mumbled and Kaapo shrugged. Across the room there was a black pot sitting next to some fresh herbs and dried meats. Hanuel opened the pot and poured the stew into a small clay bowl. Luckily it was still warm. Before taking it over he threw a handful of herbs and dried meat into it, and then handed it to Echo gingerly making sure it didn't spill. She took it from his hands with a nod of thanks.

"You know, you don't have to tend to me. I can just guilt my brother into doing things for me. He acts tough but if I can't walk and there are no witnesses around, he'll help," Echo said very matter-of-factly. Hanuel looked over at Kaapo in disbelief.

"Think again! I won't get you anything like he does, and I refuse to hold your hand as you sleep unless you are actually on your deathbed. Maybe then I'll *think* about it," Kaapo said. Echo's heart fluttered, making her breathe a little faster when she noticed Hanuel's embarrassment. With her brother in the room making his badly timed remarks it was hard for her to actually appreciate all Hanuel had done.

While he looked away in embarrassment, she drank some of her stew and then put the bowl at her bedside. She then sank into her bed and grabbed for Hanuel's hand, gently resting it on her stomach as she lay down.

"Goodnight you goon. Time to be quiet. I'd like to get some real sleep now," she said to her brother.

Kaapo snorted and turned over so he wasn't facing the two. It was obvious he was finished getting in the middle of their budding romance that was clearly hard to stomach for him. Hanuel rested his head beside Echo's body again and looked up at her. He slowly caressed her hand with his thumb, and Echo ran her other hand through his curls. She watched as his eyes closed and he smiled with relief.

THE FIRST ECHO

The next morning in the healer's hut the three young adults that had spent the night were very rudely awakened at sunrise. Eira came into the room with a rope draped over her shoulders that had eight small cast iron pans hanging from it. They were all clanking ridiculously out of tune with her footsteps as she walked across her stronghold. All three of the teenagers were wincing at the loud sounds.

"Up! Everyone up! Kaapo you let me take a look at you first." Without warning, Eira took his hand in hers with his palm facing up and she lightly stabbed him in the fleshy part of his palm with a small thorn. He bled a little, this time normally, and she nodded to herself in satisfaction as Kaapo seethed, annoyed and now in pain.

"You're free to go shifter. Now please, don't come back here for at least a day."

"I make no promises," shaking his head Kaapo got to his feet and stretched out his arms and legs as Eira walked around Hanuel to the side of Echo's bed.

"Eira please tell me you don't have to stab me too." Echo whined at the thought and Eira shook her head.

"No, but I do have to check your stitch." Both of the women eyed Hanuel which was a very big sign for him to jump up from the chair and move. The old healer took the seat Hanuel had scooted from and gingerly touched the skin around it. Echo winced but noticed she was only feeling a dull pain. It was nothing as sharp as she did yesterday.

"I want you to stay here for a little. We'll see how much pain it gives you to walk on it in a few hours. Got it?" Echo nodded in response to Eira, and Kaapo burst through the front door to get outside.

"I'm free!" he bellowed before winking back at the two, and then jogged out the door. It wasn't long until he was dragged back in by the scruff of his neck by Asmund, who was followed by Takoda and Ringwaldr. Eira rolled her eyes as they all barged into her cabin.

"Is this the new meeting place for the leading family? I wasn't told ahead of time. You know we need this space for the ill and wounded, not for your politics." She closed the door behind them all. Hanuel and Echo looked confused at the group that had come in. Kaapo was frustrated as he had so quickly lost his short-lived freedom.

"What's going on?" Echo asked slowly looking to both of her parents.

"We need to discuss your newly found ability. We've discussed it with the army's elders last night, and now we must speak with Eira. We figured since you both are already here because of your misfortune from the past few days, we could all just have a discussion," Takoda explained and then turned to Hanuel.

"Hanuel, you seemed to have seen the incident with the Harmak. Could you explain what you saw in a little more detail please?" Takoda asked Hanuel kindly. Everyone's gaze was suddenly set on Hanuel. Echo looked over at him noticing how nervous he'd suddenly become.

"Uh, I don't really know..."

"Just start from the beginning. What did you see

her do?" Ringwaldr asked. He never seemed to have the patience for anyone.

"Well... uh... we spotted the Harmak... Echo was maybe eight footsteps away from it. I blinked, and suddenly saw her with it in both of her hands, and a giant gash on her leg." Hanuel took a sharp breath in and his eyes quickly jumped to Echo then back to her mother. "There was also this green mist around her that lingers and then fades. The first time I saw her jump from one place to another it was at night, so I thought that my vision was playing tricks on me. But this time there really was a green haze around her." Hanuel tousled his hair in front of his eyes in a nervous confusion as he finished.

"So you're saying there was a green haze around her both times it happened, at night and with the Harmak?" Ringwaldr repeated slowly as his eyes burned through Hanuel's. The intense look he was getting made Hanuel gulp down and he nodded in response.

"I guess it's a bad time to say it but the night it happened was when we had caught that stranger. She escaped and we ran after her. Echo caught her by sort of lunging at her, but like I said I blinked and she was somewhere she wasn't before. Almost like she's running really fast but usually with the runners I can see them." The three adults in the room all exchanged looks.

"Eira, what do you think that coincides with?" Ringwaldr looked to the old healer who was enthralled by the conversation and still had the mysterious pans around her neck.

"I don't think there's any question Ringwaldr. I told the girl before and I'll tell you again." She looked directly at Echo as she said it. "You found that antler for a reason. You're connected to the Hirzla. There's nothing we know of in the forest that can do that. The green haze is a good clue though. The only talk of green haze was from Draviden so many years ago. It's a shame the man is dead. He's the only one who ever really saw one. His son died only a short time ago, I'd speak to his kin, Agrun, if I were you." Eira looked from the three adults to Echo, giving her an extra nod.

"That seems to be the consensus. Rythyn thought she could be displaying a Hirzla ability as well. It's common knowledge that our abilities coincide with what lives in the sacred forest. No one has ever seen what a Hirzla can really do because we can't track them. She's the answer. They can jump. Disappear and reappear." Ringwaldr looked at Echo. His emotionless speech suddenly changed. Echo caught the faintest hint of a smirk on his face.

"Echo is the only one of her kind. She is the first," Ringwaldr said slowly. A chill ran up Echo's spine. She suddenly felt herself begin to sweat from nerves. It became obvious that Hanuel wasn't the only one put on the spot now.

"Echo do you know how you're doing it?" Ringwaldr asked her very pointedly. Echo sighed and shook her head. He seemed to become more impatient by the second.

"What were you thinking when it happened? Try

giving us more detail." Everyone in the room noticed his demanding tone and Takoda's body language was telling everyone that she might jump Ringwaldr if he starts to raise his voice more than he already was.

"I don't know! The first time it happened I think I fell out of a tree! It wasn't even the night Hanuel was there. It was when we first spotted the girl!"

"There's no need to yell, Echo," Eira chimed in and Echo got even more frustrated. Why wasn't her father asking Ringwaldr to back off? He was the seer of all seers. How did he not already know the answers? His visions weren't exclusive to just what he saw. How did he not see what she was seeing when he so famously had the vision of her brother shifting?

"What are you talking about Echo? Just tell us more," Ringwaldr asked tiredly.

"I don't want to talk right now."

"Echo, please," Takoda pleaded gently, noticing that Echo was only getting worse when she heard Ringwaldr's tone.

"Echo, it couldn't hurt to just try and explain yourself. Come on," Hanuel added. Now Echo was really frustrated. It felt like the whole room was waiting for her to sprout little wings out of her back and show them a magic trick. It quickly set her off the edge and she swung her legs off her bed. Everyone jumped, ready to catch her if she fell but she seemed fine when she stood, except for the pained expression she was making.

"If none of you are going to leave me alone, I'll just go to my cabin and hide," she stated as she attempted to stomp off like a child. But she ended up wincing with every step.

"Echo I told you to wait a little until you walk!" Eira shouted at her. Takoda tried to keep her from leaving but Echo easily pushed through her parents and walked out the door.

"Well, she is her mother's daughter," Ringwaldr said under his breath. That was enough to make Takoda snap at him.

"What, you couldn't predict with that wonderful foresight of yours that your tone would make her storm out of here?"

Amidst the tongue lashing that Takoda had now begun giving Ringwaldr, Asmund nodded to Hanuel to go and bring Echo back. Kaapo was leaning against a wall sluggishly banging his head against it as he didn't want to deal with this the first day he was actually feeling better.

"Echo wait!" Hanuel yelled behind her as he chased her down the path. All she could do was hobble and she didn't get very far. "Echo, please just come back inside and rest."

"Hanuel don't you think I would've told you what I was doing if I knew?" She snapped at him as she stopped in place. There was a moment of silence before Hanuel sighed and shrugged.

"Come on Echo you can't be totally oblivious to it. I can't really believe you're not doing *something...*" Hanuel said slowly and then realized as Echo's expression changed he had maybe messed up.

"So now I'm daft? Because I'm 'oblivious' to it? Get lost! Just because you were a child prodigy like my brother doesn't mean you know everything!" Echo shoved him hard. He grabbed her wrists to keep her in place, but she easily pushed him off and continued to get away.

"Echo! I never called you daft and I never said I knew everything. I just can't believe you wouldn't find a pattern in what's happening!" Hanuel shouted and stayed in place now, but she kept hobbling away as his assumptions didn't seem to help at all.

"Leave me alone!" She shrieked back at him over her shoulder and paused as she noticed the pain in his face. It didn't change her feelings though. Everyone around her was waiting for her to do something she couldn't understand and was scared of, and the one person she thought wouldn't have expectations of her, suddenly did. That made her mad, madder than she'd ever been with him.

Back at the healer's cabin Takoda had just finished up with her thorough tongue lashing. Ringwaldr seemed unfazed by it. Everyone in the room was scared she might kill him and them too if they got too close. Eira attempted to break the silent tension that followed the screaming. She had tried to tell Takoda to settle down many times but Takoda was the only person Eira was actually scared of getting in the way of.

"Because... I don't know anything of this ability, it's best if we help Echo try to control it... before she hurts herself further. I'm not against her trying to use her ability but she needs to recover from her wound." Eira looked from Takoda and then to Ringwaldr as she said those words. "She should be fine for now. Everyone let Echo rest for a day. That girl has done much too much of your bidding lately. You're going to make her look as old as I am if you keep pestering her the way you do." Eira shot all the adults in the room a very pointed look.

"Can I go now?" Kaapo whined like a child and his mother waved him off. Without a second thought he was gone through the front door. Outside the window his parents watched him change from a man to a wild dog and back again. His roaring laughter of freedom could be heard even as he got farther from the cabin.

9
THE FIRST OF
HER KIND

The sounds of children laughing could be heard outside of Echo's door and it only upset her more. After an hour or so of moping in her bed, she still wasn't finished. She had no reason to be happy right now and she really didn't feel like pretending she was okay with everything. Ringwaldr went from ignoring her for two years to making her feel absolutely worthless, and now here he was begging her to do a trick for him as if she was his puppet. The more she thought about it the more furious she became.

As she lay in her bed and looked up at the wooden slats of her ceiling she thought about going out to climb a tree and disappear from everyone. Running away would show them, but when she sat up in her bed her leg pain reminded her that she probably shouldn't be moving too much. Startled by a knock at the door, she sighed in frustration.

"What!" she snapped.

"Let me in." Her brother's muffled voice could be heard from the other side.

"Why does it sound like you have your face pressed against the door?"

"Because I do," Kaapo responded. Echo rolled her eyes and shook her head before she limped to the door to let him in.

"Before you yell at me just hear me out." He began as he walked past her and sat on her bed. He was moving as quickly and unpredictably as usual, but there seemed to be something off about him.

"First off, you should talk to Hanuel. He feels terrible. I haven't seen him cry since he was about this high," Kaapo put a hand in the air about the height of a toddler, "but he looks pretty close to it, and I have a feeling I know why, but I'll let you deal with that. Second," Kaapo paused and took a deep breath, "it's nice to know you finally dug real deep and found out what you can do." For a moment Kaapo looked genuinely impressed by Echo and she felt like maybe this ability wasn't a complete curse like she had thought it was from the beginning. Kaapo clapped his hands, and instantly stopped the thoughtful moment. "Now, I wanna help you learn what you can do with it and forget about mom and dad and *especially* Ringwaldr right now. I'm gonna make sure you don't have to deal with them for a while. All right?" It's times like these that reminded Echo that she actually did have a caring older brother and not just an annoying one. He had a real aptitude with people. He knew what to say and how to say it to make them feel what they really needed to feel at the time. Completely ignoring the comment about Hanuel, Echo sighed and moved on.

"Where do I even start? I don't know what I'm doing. How do I figure out *how* to do it?" Kaapo got to his feet immediately, putting a hand on his hip while the other scratched his chin. After a few seconds, something hit him.

"We'll recreate a situation where it happened, for example the thing in the woods. You were near an animal and then you suddenly had it in your hands. Luckily for *you*, I can turn into animals. So, let's try!" Kaapo said excitedly and then shook his hair. The young man's head started to shrink before Echo's eyes and his body followed suit. He sprouted long white hairs and his ears started to stretch out and become taller than his head. When he sat upon the floor he was a small white bunny. Echo tilted her head at the sight.

"I don't think you're small enough," Echo said slowly and then shook her head as she motioned her hands to try and fit around the white rabbit's stomach. "Try something smaller."

The white rabbit twitched its nose and suddenly its ears wound around each other to form the head of a snake. The rabbit's fluffy body seemed to suck in the long, white hairs and before Echo's eyes they turned into the pattern of a small, green garden snake.

"No, I hate snakes. Try something else!" she

demanded. She sat on her bed quickly and brought her feet up from the ground. Even though she knew it was her brother, the mere thought of a snake in her room made her shiver and tuck herself into a little ball. Suddenly, the snake began to shrink in on itself like an accordion as it quickly began to sprout little grey hairs all over its body. Its long tail became very thin and flesh coloured, and there he sat on the floor as a mouse. Echo suddenly felt strange as if she was remembering something, but she couldn't quite put her finger on it.

"I don't want to do this." As soon as she said it Kaapo came out of his mouse form, changing so quickly back to himself on all fours on the ground that it startled Echo. When he looked like himself again he was coughing up a storm and looked as if he were about to throw up. Echo went wide-eyed and hobbled over to his side grabbing his shoulder to help support him.

"I need to wretch." With that, he ran out of the room. He missed Echo's patio steps by no less than a foot and puked in front of Sturla, the young scout that was also a shifter. Sturla ran to Kaapo's side and Echo limped over as well.

"Let me take you to Eira's friend," Sturla began with concern. Kaapo shook his head no as he pushed the young man away.

"I'm not going back there, I just left! I'll be fine," Kaapo mumbled and walked back into Echo's cabin. Echo and Sturla stood in a confused silence for a moment.

"What's with big bear?" Sturla smirked as he finally

turned to ask Echo, and Echo grinned. That was a nickname he'd given Kaapo the first night Kaapo had shifted. Sturla called the siblings Little Echo and Big bear. Echo really appreciated his light-hearted attitude, especially at a time like this.

"It's been a rough few days... he'll be fine. I hope," Echo said and Sturla nodded his head in understanding.

"Well, you know where to find me, little Echo. Give me a big shout if I need to carry him somewhere," Sturla replied.

"Thanks, friend," Echo added and gave him a quick nod before she went back into her cabin. She took a look at Kaapo who was now sitting on her bed with his head in his hands.

"Are you sure you're okay? Maybe you should just tell Eira."

"I just... smelled something weird and got ill. It's not that big of a deal."

"What? What smells?" Echo asked sniffing the air but not catching a scent of anything out of the ordinary. She could smell the forest's flora that usually wafted in through her cabin window on a gentle breeze but nothing more, and she looked confusedly to Kaapo.

"I don't know... when I changed into a mouse I just smelled something so strong I had to get away, and now I feel fine," he said as he lifted his head from his hands and looked to Echo.

"I still want to try and get you to use your ability." Kaapo scratched his head deep in thought and then cautiously continued, "What if... Hanuel, you and I go to the edge of the forest... where no one will bother us, and try?" He asked slowly, knowing he was overstepping when he said Hanuel's name and Echo's mouth tensed up. "We might need the extra help, what with me being ill and all." Kaapo tried to reason with her more and Echo sighed at his feeble attempts. Knowing him to be the stubborn type, she figured she'd give in just this once but by no means was she going to make it easy.

"I could just get Sturla. He's helpful and nice enough, and he hasn't angered me in the last day," Echo answered. Kaapo gave her a look that told her she knew what he was trying to do. It was obvious he wanted her and Hanuel to make up, probably just so he could keep teasing them, or maybe because he cared about her feelings sometimes.

"Come on, Echo." Kaapo nudged her, and she rolled her eyes.

"Fine. If you puke there I don't have to clean it up, I have one condition though," she said rather unwillingly.

"I thought the condition was that you wouldn't have to clean up my puke next time?" Echo grimaced at Kaapo's smug face after what he'd said.

"No, that's not a condition. Before we do anything else, I want to speak to Agrun."

"As long as we're getting somewhere, that's the spirit!" He responded excitedly and stood up, holding out his arm to help her walk. The two slowly made their way over to the carpenter's stronghold where Agrun would most likely be working in the day. Just at the edge of the forest, there was a large building. There were several men cutting trees on the forest's edge and another group cutting logs on stumps. When Kaapo spotted Agrun chopping wood on one of the stumps he called out to the man, making him swing and miss the piece he had placed. It was quite comical until he looked over and glared at the voice that had thrown off his aim.

"Sorry, Agrun!" Kaapo shouted. When Agrun realized it was Kaapo calling to him the man looked over at the two with concern, suddenly not caring that Kaapo had made him miss.

"Yes?" the man responded as he placed his axe down against the stump he was cutting on and then took a seat upon it. As the siblings approached, Agrun glanced at Echo's leg wound and his eyes widened. If Echo remembered correctly, the man was no more than six or seven years older than Kaapo, but he looked surprisingly young for his age. He had a short braid that ended in the middle of his shoulder blades with an undercut below. She'd never taken a good enough look at Agrun, but now as she stood quite close to him, she noticed his eyes were slightly different. They were green like her mother's, but the pupil of the left one seemed brown. If you stared at it long enough, which Echo had done, anyone would notice it was still green around the edge, but the pupil was very dilated.

She'd caught herself staring, but it seemed when she shook herself out of it so did Agrun as he was staring at the wound on her leg.

"Staring at my eye, huh? Did it when I was a child.

Got into a fight. I won't tell you what it was over, but I didn't win." He smirked, and Echo grinned awkwardly back at him before staring at her feet. She never realized he was charismatic. There was never really a chance to talk to the man until now. "Now, what can I help you both with?" he asked, this time a little impatiently. Kaapo looked over at his sister and gave her a small nudge. Echo cleared her throat and then stammered before finally getting some words out.

"Um, Agrun, if you don't mind, I wanted to ask you some questions about your grandfather. Draviden." Echo said rather quickly, realizing now that she was keeping this man from his work. Agrun looked a bit shocked for a moment then let out a short dubious laugh.

"Why would you think I know anything about him? He died before I turned six, and before that, he was the cause of most of my ridicule growing up. The man who spouted nonsense and then one day got lucky and saved our men from a cave-in." Draviden scoffed and then quickly looked away from Echo, realizing he was getting a bit hostile without trying to be.

"I'm sorry, I just wanted to know if maybe he told you more about the Hirzla that he claimed led him there, or if he kept something about the creature, maybe a recollection? Maybe your father mentioned something?" Echo's shoulders lowered in disappointment when she heard the man sigh.

"Anything of his was turned over by my father to the council, years ago. Your father would know more than

I, Echo. All I know was that he passed on that dreadful sleepwalking to my father. I'm certain that's what killed him. I found out the hard way why Eira calls it deadwalking." Echo suddenly gasped, and Kaapo looked wide-eyed at his sister. Seemingly confused, Agrun looked from one sibling to the other, "What? What is it?"

"Sleep walking, you said both your father and Draviden sleepwalked?" Echo asked.

"Yes… I'm certain he sleepwalked straight into the forest one night. Never returned. He'd done it before, but my mother or I would find him in the morning. There's no other explanation. He had no reason to leave. I was devastated."

"I'm so sorry Agrun, how is it I never heard about it?" Echo asked, concern filling her face.

"You were much too young, happened over a decade ago." Agrun waved his hand as if he were trying to shoo the memory from the air like an annoying fly, but Echo could see the pained expression on his face.

"Echo what if you sleepwalk into—"

"Quiet." Echo shot lowly at Kaapo, but it seemed Agrun had already understood the exchange.

"You sleepwalk Echo?" he asked.

"Yes… now and then." The girl shrugged and uncomfortably grabbed at her wrist that she used to tie to the bedpost as a child, ashamed. Looking back at Agrun, she noticed him squinting rather oddly at her.

"Do you see anything when you do?" Agrun asked her cautiously. Echo gulped down. In somewhat of a shock, she tried to recall a time when she sleepwalked and remembered what had happened, but in each incident, she was entirely out of it. As if she had blacked out.

"No… I can never remember what happens when I wake. I end up finding myself in a terrible situation when I do. Why do you ask?" Agrun cleared his throat and looked down at her wound again.

"It's just that," getting to his feet, he suddenly looked flustered rather than angry, "that's where his horrible visions came from, he'd tell my father about visions of war, and blackened bodies as if they had been burnt, but nothing he saw ever came true. It was just a bunch of mad ramblings." Agrun looked around wildly to make sure no one was listening in on them and then looked back to Echo. "He was deemed a blind seer. That is until he saved everyone from the cave-in. Even then some people thought he'd just gotten lucky."

"Agrun, we need you on the line!" A woman's voice resounded from the edge of the forest, and the siblings looked over, unsure of who called. Agrun knew the beckon well and looked over at the woman with a nod.

"Coming!" he shouted back and then looked back at the two teenagers. "Listen… if I could help you with any Hirzla questions, I would, but he didn't leave us with much. I'd ask your father when you get the chance. Although I can't promise he'd know much either." The siblings exchanged a look as Agrun took off to the forest.

"Does that satisfy your condition?" Kaapo asked

awkwardly, unsure if that even helped.

"I guess it'll have to for now." Echo sighed, and they headed off for Hanuel's cabin. Once they arrived Echo stood out on the path with her arms crossed over her chest squinting as she was standing in the sun.

Her brother had the honour of going up to the door and knocking. When Hanuel answered the door he looked rather ragged and he quickly tried to fix himself by shaking out his curly mane but only made it worse as he so famously did. Echo's butterflies suddenly erupted in her stomach for no reason in particular and she silently wished she had a better net for those things already.

"Hanuel, we'd like to invite you to help us figure out what Echo does to get this ability to work. If you'd so kindly join us?" Kaapo grinned his infamous grin and Hanuel looked from him to Echo, with melancholy eyes.

"As long as she's okay with it," Hanuel answered quietly as he closed the door behind him and nodded over to Echo. There was a look in his eyes that told Echo he was scared of saying something wrong to her, and Echo felt some shame when she looked at him. Maybe she was wrong for getting angry with him so quickly, but it still hurt her that he didn't believe her when she was being cornered. She rolled her eyes in frustration and started to hobble off in the direction of the forest. Her leg wasn't in any more pain than before but walking on it really wasn't helping. Kaapo rushed to her side again but she refused to have him help her now. Hanuel kept a close distance behind her and when they got into the forest he offered up a stump for her to sit on. In her defiance, she saw a log four feet away and took a seat on that instead, instantly regretting it as she almost fell backwards on it when Kaapo grabbed her hand to steady her just in time.

"All right, what do you want me to do now?" Echo mumbled embarrassed as Kaapo was very obviously trying to keep himself from laughing at the small half fall Echo just had.

"Well, I know my ability takes some thought, and Hanuel's is more like… it's just there. It's not something you can make happen or not happen. If there's a loud noise you're hearing it worse than I am? Correct?" Kaapo asked and Hanuel nodded his head slowly as he took a seat on the stump he had offered up to Echo. He looked miserable and his body language proved that he was.

"Ok so we're going to figure it takes a thought because right now you aren't… doing the thing you do? We should really have a name for it shouldn't we? What about naming it after yourself, you are the first to be able to do this… Echoing? Should we call it Echoing? Blinking seems like it would make sense too. Hanuel said he blinked and you were just in a new place. Anyone?" He looked from Hanuel and then to Echo and the two shrugged one after the other.

"Thanks for the help you two, lovely audience," Kaapo mumbled sarcastically and then continued, "I'm going to call it 'Echoing' for now. Echo do you

remember what you thought the first time you did it?"
Echo sighed and looked up at the sky. If she wasn't
having such a terrible start to her day she'd be enjoying
the beautiful sunny weather. She was sitting in a perfect
spot of shade where the sun could still kiss her skin, but
she felt a light breeze come in through the trees. She
closed her eyes and thought for a second.

"The first time… I think I was in the tree, and I
was trying to get down really quickly, and I thought I
missed a branch. I think I just… thought to myself '*Am
I falling?*'… and I was suddenly on the ground on all
fours…" Kaapo looked Echo up and down suspiciously.

"But wouldn't you have thought, *I'm going to catch
myself?*" Echo scrunched up her face.

"Well obviously, but isn't that just instinct? You
asked me what I thought in my head, not what my
first… instinct would be… huh." Slowly Echo seemed
to be putting something together in her mind. Saveria
had mentioned something about letting her instincts
kick in. She explained that when she used her ability
she would just think it and it would happen, but what
if she meant something deeper than just saying it to
yourself in your mind? What if Saveria meant she felt
it? Or did it because it was a natural reaction?

"Okay… maybe… I have to really want something to
be done for it to happen? I fall out of a tree I really want
to stop my fall. I lose someone in a forest I really want
to stop them. I see a bird I really want to catch, I catch
it."

"You have to have a really strong need in the

moment to do it?" Hanuel asked slowly and Echo nodded in response.

"Well I've got an idea but it'll sound mad." Kaapo shrugged and leaned in.

"You're not pushing me out of a tree," Echo retorted already knowing what he was going to say. Staring at her in disbelief that she'd already read his mind Kaapo sighed and then rolled his eyes.

"Ok... fine... if not a tree then maybe... The Sacred Falls? Even if you fall into it the pool is deep enough that you shouldn't hurt yourself, and Hanuel is a pretty good swimmer. He'll pull you out." Kaapo shrugged and Echo thought about it for a moment. As her heart began to race at the idea she bit her lip. It wasn't the craziest thought he'd ever had.

"Let's do it." Echo nodded and stood up, swaying just a little out of pain but looking more ready than ever.

"Is it too late to change my mind?" The rushing of the waterfall muffled the sound of Echo's naturally quiet voice shouting over it. Kaapo stood behind his sister as she stood on a rock that was at the edge of the top of the falls. It was a place that most of the tribe would jump off of into the pool to pass the time. Not many people did it anymore after someone had missed the water and perished. Peering down the falls Echo tried not to think about whoever that poor soul was. In the back of her mind she could hear her mother's voice,

171

stern and much brighter sounding than hers. It was telling her to get off the edge because this wasn't just a bad idea but also very badly thought out.

"Anytime now, Echo!" Kaapo encouraged her but even he was looking down at the jagged rocks of the falls with some fear behind his eyes. Hanuel stood at the edge of the pool at the bottom around the same area where Avila had pulled her out the night she sleepwalked into it. The memory made her tense up. Clenching her jaw and taking a deep breath, she moved her injured leg over the edge. Standing on one foot she teetered and gulped down.

"This is really foolish!" she yelled out to Kaapo, and he rolled his eyes.

"You need to stop thinking Echo. Remember what *you* said? Instinct!"

"Yeah but I'm not that smart!"

"Echo just do it!"

"But—"

Kaapo lunged at her from behind and Echo felt her stomach sink.

Weightless would be the only word to describe the feeling she had. Even though her feet never left the rock she felt herself turn into nothing but smoke, and her brother fell right through her. It took a moment for her to realize that she was still standing on the rock in one piece and her brother had been the one to dive through the air into the water. When she heard the splash she knelt down at the edge she was already close to hoping she'd see him come up. It took a moment, but the boy

172

emerged from the water yelling in triumph.

"Did you see that?" he shouted to Hanuel who had both of his hands on his head and a shocked expression on his face. Hanuel nodded slowly as he stared at Echo, still very stunned. Echo looked down at the two, confused but glad that her brother was still in one piece. She very badly hobbled down the nineteen steps she had climbed up to get where she was and met the two boys down at the side of the pool. At the bottom the water wasn't nearly as loud but they still had to raise their voices to hear each other. Kaapo had gotten out of the pool and they all stood together at the side of it.

"You saw that right Hanuel? Half of her was this green smoke that I just fell right through and the other half was just... Echo!" Kaapo shouted excitedly and then picked up Echo by the waist and spun her around. Echo flailed like a toddler to make him put her down and when he did she shoved him.

"You still pushed me! I'm not happy about that. What if I hurt myself?" Kaapo laughed and brushed her off.

"You lived didn't you? And you did it! Do you remember what you felt? Do you think you could do it again if you just tried?" The excitement in his voice sparked a slight hope in Echo, and she couldn't stay mad at him for long.

"I mean... I can try... but!" When Kaapo excitedly nodded at her and went to pick her up again she stopped him by putting both her hands up, "No more pushing me off things!" After giving him a small shove again she crossed her arms over her chest. Hanuel seemed to be in the same stunned position he had been in. He was looking up at the place where he'd seen Echo turn into smoke and then looking back down at Echo. It made her nervous to see how stunned he had become but maybe now he'd finally believe her.

"All right, no pushing, let's go back to the edge of the forest and just try to get you to do it." Kaapo squeezed some water out of his braid and wiped his drenched face. Hanuel sighed, looking to Echo, and Echo frowned at him and started to hobble off in the direction that they had all came from. The dull constant pain in Echo's leg began to nag at her. It started to sting and she had to stop for a moment to look at it.

"What's wrong?" Hanuel asked when he heard her footsteps stop behind him. It was hard to hide anything from his hearing.

"Nothing it just... it stings. I'll be fine." Echo shook her head and continued on before Hanuel could take a look at the wound himself. Kaapo looked at Hanuel and shrugged, knowing he couldn't convince Echo to stop even if he tried. When they made it back to the first clearing Kaapo jumped into action, almost too excitedly.

"Okay so, what did you feel when I pushed you? Try to recreate that sensation and think about what you thought. It's the best way to try!" Even with those encouraging words Echo sighed deeply. Closing her eyes she winced as she felt that strange dropping feeling in her stomach again. Her heart raced and she felt the same rush of adrenalin. She tried to think about where to go but her body didn't seem to want to listen to her mind and she sighed abruptly and opened her eyes.

"This feels stupid. What if it only happens when I need it to and not when I want it to?" Her disheartened tone seemed to frustrate Kaapo.

"There you are thinking again, stop thinking! Just do it!" Trying to ignore him, Echo closed her eyes again, this time the sickening feeling in her stomach was there, but she was sure it was just nausea from nerves. When she opened her eyes, she saw the same two faces looking back at her and sighed in frustration.

"This still feels stupid."

"You are so stubborn. I might actually carry you up that tree and push you out of it just for fun!" Kaapo threatened, and Echo glared at him. Hanuel crossed his arms over his chest and raised a brow at their bickering. Even though he was used to it as he'd been friends with them since they were toddlers, it still tended to get on his nerves. Hanuel took a seat on a log just behind him as he waited.

"Ugh!" Echo closed her eyes hard and tried to recreate the feeling again. All she wanted to do was hide in a tree. That's where she wanted to go. In a high tree where she could disappear and everyone would just leave her alone.

"Echo... where are you?" The familiar voice of Hanuel could be heard but it was at such a distance now that Echo couldn't place it as she still had her eyes closed. Opening them slowly she was met with green leaves and thick branches. She felt a tree branch just under her bottom and she gasped in confusion.

"I... don't know?" In bewilderment she answered back and looked down around her. Quickly she got her bearings as she spotted the forest floor. The clearing that she had just been in was behind her by two or three strides. Her brother and Hanuel were looking around confusedly on the ground. She let out a short laugh as she was impressed with herself for finally doing something she thought she had no control over. Hanuel looked up when he heard the laughter, but he still couldn't see Echo. She had 'echoed' into a tree and now she so desperately wanted to go back to where she was standing in front of the boys to prove to herself that she could do it. Quickly, Echo closed her eyes and tried to bring that feeling back, that dire feeling of falling or being pushed and having to catch herself.

In her mind's eye she was standing back in front of Hanuel and her brother, and when she opened her eyes there she was in front of them. The green hazy mist that followed her, seemed to dull down much faster when she controlled her last movement. She laughed again in excitement and the two looked back at her with wide-eyed grins. Within seconds that seemed to change as Hanuel looked down at her leg. A sharp pain ripped through the wound on her thigh and she let out a small groan as she fell to her opposite knee. Hanuel didn't catch her in time but he made sure to help her up instantly. Echo looked down at her leg and noticed the gash was bleeding as well as a light green haze was swirling around it. It seemed as if the small amount of green smoke didn't know where to go and kept swirling around the open gash.

"You know how much I don't want to say it... but I think we have to go back to Eira's." Kaapo sighed heavily and the two silently agreed. Echo let go of Hanuel and struggled to stand. Hanuel rolled his eyes at her persistence to push him away but backed off. Walking back to Eira's took longer than it should have. Echo was in so much pain now that any pressure she put on the leg seemed to halt her movement completely. Every time she would stop, Hanuel would give her a look as if to say he was ready to catch her at any moment.

"Would you just let one of us carry you?" Kaapo yelled back at her as he was the furthest ahead. Echo angrily shook her head no. When she stumbled again, only moments later, Hanuel swiftly picked up the stubborn girl, cradling her with ease like a honeymooner over a threshold. Echo crossed her arms over her chest in silent protest but decided against arguing. What she really wanted to do was thank him but her hold on this grudge was far too strong.

19
THE
COMPENDIUM

"You three again?" Drained, Eira shook her head in disbelief at the sight of the three teenagers entering her cabin for the umpteenth time in three days.

"Believe me, I don't want to be back here but Echo's leg looks rather odd." Kaapo hopped onto the bed he had been in and out of for the past three days and crossed his arms over his chest. Hanuel gently placed Echo down on the bed next to Kaapo. Echo gulped down and wanted to say thank you but her pride made her hold it in. It was hard to hold onto a grudge against Hanuel when he was caring for her so much but she still managed to do it with that hard head of hers.

"Well let me have a look." Eira sat next to Echo's bed and her eyes widened.

"It really hurts."

"How long has that green haze been there?" Eira

asked slowly as if she were afraid she would sound crazy for pointing it out. "It is there right? We're all seeing that? My funny eye isn't just playing tricks on me is it?" She looked around at the two boys and they both nodded in agreement.

"I… did that thing… and then my leg started to really hurt and well… now I'm here." Echo sighed, knowing how stupid that sounded. Injured and reckless, she imagined those are the words her mother would use to scold her if she got the chance.

For a few moments Eira was uncomfortably close to Echo's leg, inspecting it as if it were a puzzle she had yet to solve. Suddenly, she got up from the chair and shuffled across the floor to her table. From the shelves, she pulled down a giant leather-bound book full of loose writing skins with scribbles and scratches all over them.

"What is that thing?" Not being one to sit still, Kaapo had gotten up and followed behind Eira, giving her a small spook when he asked the question as he was standing just behind her shoulder.

"Boy! I have been on this earth for sixty-four years. It's not difficult to kill me with a quick fright. Don't do that!" she snarled and whacked him in the shoulder with her book as she walked over to Echo's bed. Eira threw down the large binder of scattered papers next to Echo making the girl jump, and then she grabbed a piece of charcoal from the side table. The minute she sat back down she began scratching furiously on a particular piece of dried buckskin. The three young adults leaned in to see if they could distinguish what she was writing. With no luck, Echo waited in frustration.

"What is that and what are you doing?"

"Shhh!" Eira shot without looking up as she finished writing a few more words and then set her attention on Echo.

"This... is my compendium. Everything I've ever discovered in my life about the sacred Forest and its creatures is in this book. I must record what I can in it when I see something new... and you darling, are something else." Echo looked down at the page.

THE FIRST ECHO

The symbols made Echo feel uneasy. The Hirzla antler seemed to have been drawn recently, and there was also a small scribble of what looked to be the shape of a young girl walking with her eyes crossed out. When Echo's eyes uncomfortably lingered on that drawing Eira noticed.

"That was when I recorded you finding the stag, and that's when I recorded your most recent deadwalk. I think they're connected, but I don't know why, this is why I write things down." Echo sighed and laid back on the bed. It seems Eira had already figured out what she'd gone to speak to Agrun about. Her leg pain seemed to get better slightly as she lay there, but she could still feel it stinging when the green haze decided to wisp around more uncontrollably than it had before. The two boys seemed to take a little more interest in the book, and of course Kaapo was the first to ask.

"What's in that book about me?" he asked with a raised brow as he leaned against the table, staying a safe distance away from Eira now.

"You, my dear, are a shifter, connected to the sacred forest by wild sigoons, or more commonly known as 'wigoons'... the children tend to call them that. When you first changed into a mountain bear and a boodhound I had written you into the shifter page, but then, you changed into a snake, and a coyote, and... oh dear what was it?"

"Blue jay." Everyone cringed when Kaapo said it as they remembered the time he shifted into a bird to try and impress a girl named Undra. He had asked her what her favourite animal was and then changed into it. When he flew up, he was very unfamiliar with the feeling of wings and got caught in her hair so badly she didn't speak to him for several months after.

"Yeah I know, I know, it wasn't my finest moment," Kaapo mumbled and Eira sighed before continuing.

"Anyway, when you showed me that you were the very rare case of someone having more than one shift, your page turned into a mess. Over the years I've tried to keep up with all your shifting, but you've had so many, I stopped keeping track! I don't know how you do it but everything you and others have ever tried to explain to me is written in this book." Eira then turned to Hanuel with a raised brow. His curious look back at her was enough to tell her to continue. "Hanuel, you are the best of the bloodhounds to the present day, my dear. The forest scavengers. You, like your great grandfather, were gifted with their sight, *and* hearing. Most of our people are only born with one or the other, like your father Rythyn and his impeccable sight even in the dark. Ever since you were young I knew there was something different about you. Crying when your mother would cut your hair shorter than it is now because you used your magnificent curls as ear covers when noise became too much. I don't know why you developed your ability before becoming a man. That is very uncommon, and you've never seemed to be able to turn it off. Even when I tried to help you. Only a few in our tribe can. I remember one day when you caught me cursing under my breath and your father had a good word with me to be careful with what I say around you after you repeated it in front of him." Eira smirked and shook her head. "What was it you told me not too long ago? The noises can be dulled but never stopped?"

Hanuel took a shaky breath in and nodded. It seemed he was remembering something that made him antsy.

"Yes… I can hear everything all the time. Heart beats used to be like hammering to me. That has since dulled… I can tell the difference between people's breathing, and…" Hanuel's eyes shifted quickly from Echo to Eira and then he looked down at his feet. It seemed like he was going to continue but he just stopped and ruffled the hair on the top of his head so it covered his eyes a little more as he looked down.

"Okay, so what you're saying is you've never seen this before. What do I do about it?" Echo finally shot, feeling a little selfish for cutting in but her worry was warranted considering her leg was glowing and the pain wasn't dying down.

"I don't want to put anything on it. I'm going to let it do what it's going to do. After all we are natural born healers as long as we're taking care of our bodies, but I will warn you now. If you can't contain yourself, I'll make sure you stay here like your brother. I thought you'd be the one I didn't have to worry about going rogue Echo." Closing her giant book of loose papers with a quick slam Eira picked it up and hobbled back over to the shelf. Kaapo took it from her gingerly and put it back up on the shelf in the hopes that she wouldn't land another whack on his shoulder.

"I don't know about you two but I'm starving. Maybe you just need some food in you?" As Kaapo walked to the front door he opened it and nodded out of it to Hanuel and Echo. "We'll find a good spot by the bonfire and get some food. I feel like people will really enjoy seeing that strange green thing in your leg." Looking down Echo let out a quick sigh and swung her legs off the bed to stand. This time when Hanuel offered a hand to help she actually took it. Realizing her defiance was no excuse for foolishness and getting help seemed to relieve the pain.

"Did you need me to carry you again?" Hanuel asked, genuinely concerned. Echo shook her head no meekly. Still ashamed she hadn't thanked him when he'd done that the first time. She was curious to know now what he had wanted to say before when she cut him off. She briefly wondered if now would be an awkward time to ask. Echo held onto Hanuel's arm for support as she limped out of the cabin and down the pathway. The three found a good seat next to the fire and Hanuel and Kaapo lined up to receive a plate of roast. As usual Hanuel jumped in front of Sturla and his friend Daes this time. The three young men had a theatrical faceoff in line that made others around them jokingly encourage them to fight. When they took fighting stances against each other, Sturla instead spread his arms out for a hug from Hanuel, and they hugged. As Sturla hugged his friend, he turned him around so Hanuel was then standing behind Sturla in line. When

THE FIRST ECHO

Hanuel realized what had happened to him he frowned over at Echo, who was watching the entire scene with a smug little smile. After Hanuel had gotten some food to bring over for Echo, people suddenly started noticing her glowing leg.

It made everyone who sat around them start having conversations about their special abilities. Sturla seemed to be the proudest of Echo, almost matching Kaapo's excitement when he heard she had finally found out she had an ability. Then Kaapo began talking about his shifting and went into great detail about how sick he had been after shifting when he was injured. Everyone was hanging on to his words because he knew how to tell stories with such colourful language. He began telling everyone he fought a stag and showed them his back injury. Echo scoffed but didn't have the heart to correct his story as he was caught up in it.

After he finished his longwinded tale, the young guarding scouts Sturla and Daes spoke with Kaapo about shifting as they all had that in common. Sturla could shift into a coyote, and Daes into a raven. Daes was newer at it though and his shift wasn't as reliable. They spoke to each other for a couple of hours. Echo listened in, completely enthralled by the way they explained some of the experiences they had when they shifted.

As the conversation slowly came to an end the bonfire died down. Kaapo started to feel ill and thought he should leave to his cabin before he lost his dinner in front of everyone like he had done earlier in front of Sturla. After he'd relayed the information to his sister, Hanuel hesitantly asked Echo if she wanted him to walk her back to her cabin. When she nodded in acceptance, he seemed to light up a little.

Quietly, they made their way to Echo's cabin. Echo was still gripping tightly onto Hanuel's arm as they walked up the cabin path at sunset. Neither of them dared to speak a word to each other, Hanuel being too scared to upset Echo further. By this time Echo was just ashamed she had been so mad in the first place, seeing now that Hanuel may have just misjudged the situation and was trying extremely hard to make up for it.

When the two finally got to Echo's cabin door Hanuel gave her a nod and began to walk off. Echo gulped down and decided she was going to be the first to finally say something.

"Thank-you Hanuel and… I'm sorry." Hanuel stopped in his tracks and turned back around to her slowly, then took a few steps back towards her.

"Me too," he mumbled, unable to look her in the eyes as he ran a hand through his hair. Echo furrowed her brows and smirked at his somewhat feeble attempt at an apology.

"You too… what?" Crossing her arms over her chest and looking over at him quite smugly she tapped her foot in feigned impatience. Hanuel grinned back at her and sighed.

"I'm… sorry too," he finished. Echo uncrossed her arms and reached over for her porch to sit on the steps. When she got comfortable, she patted the space beside her so he would join her. He walked over and took a seat.

"What were you going to say before I interrupted you at Eira's?" Echo asked softly, remembering how nervous it had made him to talk about it then. She noticed those same nerves come back by the look on his face.

Hanuel looked over at her for a moment then back at his feet. He was never like this around her. He usually had the unwitting confidence of her brother without the terrible impulse. The last time she saw him struggle for words is when he kissed her.

"The conversation we were having at Eira's, it just reminded me of when we were in the forest yesterday... when you were hit," Hanuel began and mustered up the courage to look her in the eyes again. "You stopped breathing." Echo was taken aback a little. She hadn't noticed that, and it only occurred to her now that it was something Hanuel would notice, even though he had said it in Eira's cabin, Echo never really put that together. "It was only for a little... but I swear in that time... I thought about how..." Echo's brow furrowed. She was listening to him so intently that her eyes became dry from not blinking as she stared at him. "I thought about how I would feel if I never heard you breathe again." He took a quick, sharp breath and breathed out deeply just as quick. "It wasn't a very nice feeling. I've heard it every day for a lifetime. After everyone's heartbeats dulled down, and I could stand that noise... I don't remember a day I haven't heard you breathe Echo... except for yesterday." Hanuel gulped down and looked at his feet again. Echo watched as he picked up a rock and threw it across the path flippantly. She took the hand he used to throw the rock in hers. When Hanuel looked to her again she couldn't stop herself from kissing him. Baffled, it took a minute for him to really lean into it, but when he did Echo could feel just how much he cared for her.

"Gross." A familiar, whiny voice said and the two detached from the mouth to look over in the direction of the unwelcomed comment. "There's a room right behind you, use it! Also thanks, you couldn't have done that while we were scouting? Jillik and I already lost the bet to Manson." Saveria huffed and then smirked with a wink at Echo. Sighing, Echo rolled her eyes, only now noticing how hard her heart was beating. The sunset had turned into darkness and Saveria was the fire bringer set with the task of checking to make sure all the torches were still lit strongly enough to last the night.

"I'm... do you want... maybe... I don't mind if you..." Echo stumbled over her words as she pointed to her cabin behind her.

"I'll stay," Hanuel said instantly, almost as if it wasn't ever really a question. She grinned at his enthusiasm and then motioned for him to help her up. The two went into Echo's cabin. As enthused as they were to continue kissing, they both realized just how tired they were when they curled up beside each other and fell fast asleep.

THE FIRST ECHO

✖

The fog that engulfed Echo's mind was thick and green.

Wherever she turned all she could see were clouds of it. They wisped and glowed as she felt that all too familiar sinking feeling in her stomach.

Then, a wind, as strong as the feeling she had when she knocked down that redheaded monster suddenly hit her.

She was in the air, above the trees of the sacred forest.

Screaming, she came to the realization that she wasn't going to fall, she was flying, like a Harmak above the clouds.

The green, ever changing clouds. Even though she wasn't falling directly down she did feel like she was gliding to the ground.

The weightlessness felt nice until the gliding changed into falling.

Echo looked to the ground below her that she was heading for. There was a war beneath her.

Hordes of men and women fighting each other as she came falling to the earth in the middle of them.

THUD.

Her feet hit the ground and suddenly the fighting paused.

All around her people stood frozen in time as she shielded her face with both of her arms, scared they might start attacking her.

When she noticed no one was moving she looked around.

Familiar faces of her tribe's people came into view.

The enemy was unclear though.

Simply dark shapes of men with no facial features or colours.

Just bodies, void of any personification.

> *"Don't take your eyes off him."*

A husky voice she didn't recognize resounded through her mind.

> *"Don't take your eyes off him."*

The words kept repeating themselves getting louder and louder, layering themselves on top of each other, making it seem as if the one voice repeating the words, turned into many.

THE FIRST ECHO

"Don't take your eyes off him."

As the words continued, they slowly seemed to wake up the frozen bodies around her.

"DON'T TAKE YOUR EYES OFF HIM."

As they began to fight each other Echo was shoved from behind and fell forward straight into a pile of mud.

When she hit the ground it felt like she had fallen on someone's body but she slowly came to the realization that she was not in her cabin anymore lying with Hanuel. The grass was damp and smelled of fresh dew. Echo's leg throbbed as she slowly opened her eyes to take in her surroundings. Squinting at what little daylight she could see, she opened her eyes enough to notice she was behind a cabin. It looked like it was dawn, and she could hear birds chirping in the distance. Groaning, she lifted herself from the ground. She let out a sharp gasp of pain as she got to her feet. She checked her wound to make sure it wasn't bleeding or doing anything else funny, and was surprised when she noticed the green haze had finally stopped whipping around her wound. While looking down at her leg she noticed the Hirzla blade strapped to her calf. Shaking her head in confusion at the sight, she hadn't remembered falling asleep with that strapped to her. In fact, she remembered her mother taking it off when she was rushed to Eira's cabin for the wound on her leg. Echo shrugged it off and used all the strength she had in her sore body to get to the front of the cabin only to notice it was Ringwaldr's.

How did I even get here? Echo scolded herself in her mind for ever coming near this cabin. Why on earth would she have sleepwalked here? Then something suddenly hit her. This wasn't the first time this had happened. Echo took the hint that maybe something was leading her here for a reason.

Carefully, she snuck around to the side of the cabin where a window was opened and leaned in closer to hear the muffled voices.

"When that happens, he'll have nothing to believe in. I'm too important for this to fail." Ringwaldr's voice was low and he spoke slowly.

"But the girl doesn't even know what she's capable of yet. Are you convinced this vision will happen soon?" Avila sounded unsure of herself.

"Soon enough. It keeps coming to me. She will slaughter many. In the beginning, it is muddy, I am unsure if she has the strength, but for this battle… I saw her kill at least ten on her own. She moves like smoke amongst them and when she cuts their throats, they don't even have time to think about what she's doing."

Echo stood frozen in absolute horror. There was no one else he could be talking about but her. What Ringwaldr was explaining sounded like Echo, but it wasn't who Echo wanted to be. Her heart and mind filled with a panic she had never known before. She hugged herself, so uncomfortable with the thought of slitting at least *ten* men's throats? Had she heard that right? That wasn't her. It couldn't be. In disbelief, she started walking back to her cabin, but when she noticed people were coming out of the surrounding cabins now, she had the sudden urge to get away from everyone.

What if she was a monster just waiting to attack? What if there was something deep and visceral in her just waiting to unleash itself? She didn't understand her ability, and barely had any control over it yet; what if it ended up controlling her in a way she didn't want?

She walked off into the forest as quickly as her injury would let her, completely ignoring the nagging pain in her leg telling her to sit down as it slowly became worse. She found a tree off the path in the forest and tried to climb up it. Her weakness proved to be too much, though, and she slipped and fell backward, catching herself on her elbows. Letting out a groan in frustration she got to her feet and limped to the tree trunk again. Leaning on it for support, she breathed deeply and started up it. This time her arms did more of the work to lift herself. Climbing the tree still proved to be an enormous struggle, with the amount of pain in her leg, she ended up giving up and just sitting at the base of it.

Echo didn't exactly have a plan, but she knew she couldn't hurt anyone this far into the forest. The past week she had proven to herself that she had no idea what she was capable of and that scared her. There was no way she would be going anywhere near anyone she cared about after hearing that she could easily slit their throats. The last few days had made her lose her entire grip on what she knew to be. Now that she was hearing her father's highly esteemed seer say she was a killer it made her want to be sick. It seemed whatever he said did happen, and it all came down to that awful antler she'd found in the woods. At this point, she knew that it was a curse. She wished she had never picked it up in the first place. Looking to the blade, she pulled it out and looked sickly at it. What if it was this thing that was doing this to her? What if she had left it where it was in the first place? Would all of this be happening now?

Her eyes focused on the blade, but when they unfocused for a moment, they noticed the green haze that surrounded the base of her tree, making her stare in confusion. Wispy green clouds multiplied around her and she gulped down before she put the knife back into her sheath. Even though she had planned to throw it away, something told her she might want to hang on to it for a little longer.

No, not again, please not again.

She thought to herself as she lifted her knees to her chest and held them tightly. She burrowed her head into her knees and closed her eyes. What she couldn't see couldn't hurt her right? Echo scoffed at her foolishness and slowly opened her eyes in the hopes that they were playing tricks on her, and the green mist would be gone. That was too much to ask for though, because there it was still lingering in the air. She was faced with a choice now. Try to climb up the tree again and get as far away from this mist as she could or follow the trail that it was so quickly making into the forest. A sudden rustle in the bushes ahead of her caught Echo's attention, and she noticed a glimpse of something. It was white and green.

Is that what I think it is?

Manson had told her once, when hunting, trying to follow a buck or doe is challenging, they blend in with the forest so well. Sometimes all you can see is their whitetail. Something told Echo what she caught a glimpse of wasn't any regular buck or doe. A green mist clouded the whitetail that looked like smoke. A pull in her heart got her to her feet, using the tree to support her.

With cautious steps, she proceeded to follow the haze. As she would walk into a green cloud, the mist would quickly fall to the ground and dispel. Her nerves made her think something was going to jump out at her. Every once and a while, she would hear a small crack of branches underneath feet that weren't hers. The sound was coming from in front of her, and she kept following it. The haze led to a camp in the forest that startled Echo at first.

She thought perhaps this was someone's home, but the fire had been doused in water to be put out, and there were bone scraps left around it. With further investigation, Echo realized this was a human-made camp, and wondered for the life of her why this would be here. For a moment, Echo looked into the trees. As she caught a glimpse of antlers through the trees, her heart began to beat faster. They were uneven. The green mist that led her there suddenly sparked a defiant green glow. She heard a low hum that began to get louder and louder until she looked to the source. Her eyes locked on to a tree, immediately the humming stopped, the mist fell to the earth and dispelled.

Scratched into the bark of the tree at eye level was a symbol Echo had only seen once before. The stranger, she had it marked on her wrist.

11 THE INEVITABLE

"Kaapo! Wake up! Have you seen Echo?" Hanuel yelled through the boy's door, and proceeded to pound on it in a rhythmically challenged fashion.

"What? No!" Kaapo rolled himself off the side of his cot and tiredly dragged himself to the door. When he opened it he noticed how anxious Hanuel looked. "If she's not in her cabin maybe she's at Eira's?" Kaapo shrugged and Hanuel shook his head no. Apparently he had already been there. Scratching his head and heaving a sigh Kaapo thought about where else she could be.

"So you went to her cabin and she just wasn't there?"

"No." Hanuel brushed at his ears. He was hearing something strange but it was like an agitating low hum. He couldn't place it, and right now while he was worried, he hadn't the time to think about it. "I stayed over last night and I woke up with her not there. I know she sleepwalks. She did it as a kid."

"First of all, I don't want to know about who sleeps with my sister. Second, yeah I just remembered Eira said she was deadwalking again. I don't want to scare you but the first place you should be checking are the sacred pools. You go there and I'll keep checking around here. Also, why do you keep touching your ears?" Kaapo looked at Hanuel in an odd way as the boy kept ruffling his hair.

"I don't know, it's like a pack of bees or something." Wide-eyed, Hanuel realized he was wasting time when Kaapo had just mentioned Echo might have sleepwalked into water. He ran for the forest and Kaapo quickly shut the door to dress and join him on the hunt for Echo.

As Hanuel came close to the edge of the forest the low humming sound seemed to get louder. Before reaching the edge of the forest, he came to a quick halt. Now he could make out the sound. It was breathing. Breathing he had never dulled out before. An indiscernible number of heartbeats he'd never heard, all beating at the same time. It was the sounds he heard as a child, when he didn't know how to dull them out. He went wide-eyed as two men slowly emerged from the trees. These were men he didn't recognize. Their faces were painted with mud and their unwelcoming glare told Hanuel they weren't there for a friendly visit. The young man backed up slowly and then took off as one of the two men lunged for him.

"Intruders! Wake up! Intruders!" Hanuel yelled as

loud as he could as he ran up the path to Hemera. As he ran he looked back at the treeline. More men and women with the same painted faces and dark green robes emerged from the brush, making him fall to his knees on the path and then get up immediately. With an unsuspecting calm a few of Hemera's people emerged from their cabins, awaking with the morning light. Mostly older farmers and carpenters were all startled by the commotion.

About thirty or more foreign men and women came running from the trees and started grabbing those who had left their cabins. The captured or grabbed were flailing and fighting. These people were smarter than they looked. They'd attacked the camp on the side that was furthest from the soldiers' stronghold. Most of this side of the Hemeran tribe were working folk, but they all had their own way of protecting themselves with their many abilities. It was just a little harder for those who didn't spend their day training in combat. Many water bringers and fire bringers did all they could with small bursts of fire and water to the face or the more delicate regions of their attackers, but there was only so much you could do to keep others at bay when your abilities weren't as reliable as you wanted them to be.

Hanuel ran straight for Asmund's and Takoda's, but the two leaders were already barrelling down the path toward the commotion. Hanuel's father, Rythyn, and three other strong men followed behind their leaders. The four giant muscular men, the biggest being Asmund, were instantly pulling the foreigners off of their tribesmen and women, pinning them to the ground, and watching as Takoda conjured up vines to strap the strangers down. Even though her skill was hard to master, she mustered up those vines quite quickly, and they moved on to more men attacking their tribe's people.

The attackers seemed much too aggressive this time. It was apparent they were trying to capture whoever they could grab, but it seemed like they didn't care who they brutally harmed in the process.

Out of breath and bewildered Echo emerged from the trees. She focused on the chaos along the path. She began running up it now, even with the stabbing pain in her leg. She saw many of her tribe's people keeping the violent foreigners at bay with their abilities, and noticed her father further along the path sitting on one of the men as her mother was effortlessly conjuring up vines in all directions.

Closest to her was a water bringer named Kanga. She had held up her hands kneeling in front of her little boy as he hid just behind her. There was a male attacker viciously trying to grab her little boy who was crying inconsolably. The sight drove Echo mad. She ran at him at full force pushing him to the ground. It was barely enough to keep him down because he bounced back and came straight for Echo. The foreign feeling of a heavy weight surprised her as he jumped on her and she fell back.

The stranger's hands wrapped around her throat. Before she could understand what was going on, she was gasping for air trying to pry his vice grip off of her. In the few seconds that felt like minutes he spent strangling her, the world seemed to slow down. She could hear her heart beating in her ears, with every beat, a new fear would come flashing into her mind.

Where's Hanuel?

Is Kaapo hurt?

If I die right now, what will happen to Kanga and her boy?

Why are these people trying to kill us?

She took a good look into her attacker's eyes, searching them for answers. It was alarming when she noticed they mirrored her fear. If he was so frightened, what was he doing? When her feeble attempts at pulling his hands off of her didn't work, she dug her nails into the right side of his face just close enough to his eye. He quickly took her hand off his face, but in the second she got to breathe she reached for the knife on her calf. When she grabbed it, she plunged it into his left arm, and he screamed out in pain. The world seemed to move faster again. The heartbeat that had started in her ears was drowned out by the sounds of fighting. When he let go of her neck to grip his arm with the other, Echo felt that sinking feeling in her stomach and was suddenly standing behind him.

She hesitated.

Something inside her told her to take the knife out of his arm and cut his throat while she stood there. Instead she ripped the knife out of his arm and whacked him upside the head with the back of her

Hirzla blade. The man collapsed.

"Echo!" Hanuel shouted as he shoved two men off of him but was being pulled by another behind him. Echo turned around to see Hanuel further up the path. Even with all the adrenaline rushing through her veins, there was another steady dosage on its way. He was being pulled at by three hooded figures and although he was holding them off mostly by kicking at them, they had already made his mouth bleed. Echo glared at the men and forced that sinking feeling into her stomach.

She ended up ramming right into one of the caped men with her left shoulder. The man in particular had a tight grip on Hanuel's arm. The move was quite clumsy, and she ended up falling but her strategy still worked. The stranger was sent tumbling to the ground. Immediately, Hanuel grinned and with that one free arm he punched out the man to his right who was so adamant on getting him. The third one that had a grip on him immediately let go and backed away as Hanuel moved forward.

This one was weaker willed than the others. As Hanuel moved forward to trap him the screaming and jostling noises all at once came to a halt as everyone heard a low grumble. Almost every head turned toward the sight of a very large mountain lion slowly walking up the path. It let out a loud roar and when everyone caught sight of the animals behind it, the foreigners seemed confused. There was a raccoon and a fox on either side of the mountain lion, and a ferret following behind. While the young stranger was distracted

THE FIRST ECHO

Echo and Hanuel both tackled him to the ground and Hanuel sat on him while Echo grabbed some rope from the outside of a nearby cabin to tie his hands with.

The mountain lion alone was intimidating enough to make most of the caped men jump back. When the mountain lion jumped through the air at someone readying to fight it, it turned into a thin garden snake as it landed, wrapping around its enemy's legs and tripping him which sent him hurtling to the ground. When the man was struggling to grab the snake around his feet, the snake turned into Kaapo and he pinned the man down, hollering over to his mother for vine rope to help him.

The remaining group of intruders witnessed the scene and exchanged looks with each other amidst the fighting. One of them let a sound escape his mouth that alerted all the others that they were fleeing and they began to run off into the trees. The few that had been captured by the strong men and Takoda were slowly escorted to the soldiers' stronghold where they would be thrown into cells. Some soldiers went to follow the escaping foreigners into the trees but Asmund yelled to them to stay put. Takoda came around to collect the one man that Echo and Hanuel had captured and used her vines as a chain to attach all of the intruders together.

There were injured tribespeople everywhere Echo looked. The intruders' feeble attempt at what seemed to be a kidnapping went horribly for them, but left everyone shaken. Echo didn't have any time to think about anything before she heard her father's booming voice again. Naturally, he was much softer spoken, but when he was angry he knew how to project.

"Soldiers, check the perimeter, do not chase anyone past the pools! We had two shifters posted on the east side at sunrise! If they didn't alert us that means there is something wrong!" Asmund pointed to his soldiers and two runners of the tribe who sped off to check the forest line where the two men that Asmund mentioned should have been posted. "Where is Ringwaldr?" Asmund bellowed. It was the first time in Echo's life that she had heard her father speak the man's name in such a tone. Anger didn't even begin to explain the emotion that seemed to fill Asmund.

The man who tangoed with time came walking up the path, his emotionless face never changing. Echo couldn't tell where he had come from. "Where were you amidst this? You've warned us of attacks before! Are you deliberately trying to ruin us or have you become blind?" Completely unprepared, Ringwaldr fell to the ground when Asmund shoved him. Usually Asmund could control his strength, but Echo had a feeling he'd done that on purpose. Angrily the man got to his feet and brushed himself off.

"No one was killed. I told you any form of attack that is not dire…"

"Asmund!" A man's voice wearily called out from the forest line.

A flock of birds were sent soaring from the treetops of the forest surrounding Hemera at the sound of a woman's blood curdling scream. The woman ran straight for the forest's edge. One of the runners that Asmund had called before, Hega was struggling to get up the path. Echo looked at the horrid sight. The young shifter named Sturla lay motionless in runner's arms.

Echo had never seen a dead body before.

It made her skin crawl.

She felt sick.

The young man who called her little Echo was just like another brother to her. A friend who always seemed to be there. She remembered seeing the young man at the bonfire so many times, lively and vibrant. It was beyond imaginable to see him like this. Echo couldn't even remember the last time she had seen Sturla without a smile on his face. As his mother cried inconsolably over him Asmund's anger finally boiled over.

He turned to Ringwaldr, the man who never seemed to waver in his emotions was coming close. His eyes widened just a little at the sight of the dead young man and for some reason, Ringwaldr turned to look at Echo.

By his silence, Asmund concluded that Ringwaldr hadn't foreseen this. The second male that was on post, Daes, walked back carefully from the forest with his arm around the second runner, Toff. He had been horribly beaten, barely able to stand or keep his swollen eyes open. Men from the tribe who had been watching the scene between Asmund and Ringwaldr had rushed over to help Toff carry Daes straight to Eira's.

"Is it dire yet Ringwaldr?" Asmund asked him in a feigned calm, rage hidden just behind his words.

"Well... it isn't one of your heirs, is it?" Ringwaldr snarled in retort, and Asmund had suddenly had enough. He bellowed in frustration and grabbed Ringwaldr by the scruff of his neck. Dragging him off in the same direction as the intruders to throw him into a cell.

When the chaos died down, everyone who was outside looked to one another in the uncomfortable silence that only seemed to break every few seconds when Sturla's mother cried out. Everyone slowly came closer to circle around them. Echo's eyes started to swell with tears and looking to Hanuel she noticed his had as well. Sturla was twenty-two years old. Everyone knew him and was close with the young man in some way. He was part of their community. Echo hugged Hanuel tightly around the waist, and he held her hard as he quietly sobbed into her neck. Sturla's mother's sobs weren't getting any better and many women of the tribe surrounded her, trying their best to console her. Hanuel let go of Echo gently when he noticed two other young men started to lift Sturla carefully. He went over to help carry the young man's body to the place where they prepared the dead.

THE FIRST ECHO

Echo went around asking everyone if they were all right, and if there was something she could get them. Most of them let her know Kaapo had come around to ask the same question, and they appreciated the siblings' help. Her tribe was spread into small groups along the cabin path, each caring for each other's wounds, big or small. Parents consoled their crying children, and family members held each other as they looked bewildered.

"Everyone, at noon we will meet at the pit. As of right now, we have to find out what these intruders were trying to do. We are all very angry about what has happened, and we will have justice for our young tribe's man. But first, we need to ensure our safety," Asmund bellowed as he came back to the group of people from the soldiers' stronghold.

When he arrived, he was swarmed. Everyone was asking him questions, looking to their leader for answers and advice. Echo saw this as her chance. There was something going on. Even if Ringwaldr wasn't going to tell her what it was. She needed to ask him. Why had he looked at her in distress? She needed to look him in the eyes, and try and understand what exactly he thought he was doing.

As quick as her injured leg would let her, she snuck behind the cabins, straying from the path where no one would see her, and limped over to the soldiers' stronghold. With three heavy knocks on the door, she was greeted by Hanuel's father Rythyn, leader of the Hemeran army. Rythyn looked exactly like Hanuel, only with lines around his eyes, straight slicked black hair with a few greys sprouting out, and a more muscular build.

"Echo, did your father send you?"

"Yes." She lied, but it seemed to work. The large man nodded for her to pass him at the door and he closed it behind her.

"He said you'd be here to see him. I thought maybe he had gone completely mad. I'm aware of just how much you dislike the man," Rythyn mumbled and walked her over to one of the locked rooms. He then lifted the large piece of wood from the deadbolt in the door, and swung it open. Echo looked inside to see Ringwaldr sitting on the floor. One of his legs was sprawled and the other was bent as he rested his elbow on it. The cell was dark. Only a small slit of daylight came through a thin rectangular cut out in the wall at the highest point of it. This was the wall Ringwaldr was sitting against. The man stared up at her, a cold lifeless expression that was no different than it ever was. Rythyn closed the door behind her but left it unlocked.

"Holler if you need me," he grunted through the closed door and Echo sighed heavily.

"I guess you're not surprised I'm here," Echo began, and Ringwaldr smirked maliciously, nodding as he did so.

"No Echo. I'm not surprised you're here. You're right on time."

"I don't have the patience to hear you speak in riddles. I want to know why you looked over at me. Like you had missed something..." Echo's heart raced. He made her blood boil. Every nerve in her body wanted to slap some sense into him, but how dissatisfying would that be? He would just show that never wavering emotionless face of his even if she did.

"For every choice you make, Echo... darling."

"Don't!"

"All right, fine." He huffed with a grin. "For every choice you make, I see, or rather my mind's eye sees several possibilities. Then, when I mull them over. I feel a certain pull to which one will happen. You... have a way of constantly keeping me on my toes." He smirked and shook his head. The strange change in behaviour made Echo slightly uncomfortable and she leaned against the door, crossing her arms over her chest.

"Am I supposed to know what that means?" Echo asked flippantly, clearly tired of his games. Ringwaldr got to his feet slowly. Echo didn't blink as she watched him, not necessarily afraid of him, but completely unsure of what he would do next.

"You have the potential to be very powerful Echo. I've seen it. In fact, if you were good at timing, and had already realized your power, Sturla wouldn't be dead right now." Echo gulped down and stared into his eyes unblinking.

"Are you saying you saw me help Sturla but were daft enough not to tell me what to do?"

"Would you have listened to me regardless?" Ringwaldr raised a brow, genuinely asking the question they both already knew the answer to. Echo was just too ashamed to say it.

"You told my brother exactly what to do before the moment our scouts were attacked by that mountain bear, but when it comes to me, you can't give me a warning! Whether or not I'd believe you!" Infuriated, Echo was trying not to raise her voice but it wasn't working.

"There is a vision much further ahead that made me not tell you what to do. And I'll say it again. I know you wouldn't have listened. In my visions of telling you myself, you practically disappear into thin air! You wouldn't have even been here for the fight, and your precious Hanuel would have been the one to cry over!"

Echo gulped down and glared at him, trying with all her might to develop the ability to just burn his skin with her eyes. What was a seer if the visions he had didn't really come true? *Nothing but a mad rambling man,* Echo thought to herself.

"Today did not go as I thought it would, and you are the underlying factor that keeps changing my visions. Time and time again you screw something up and lead us on another timeline. There is no consistency and I cannot figure out why." The man heaved a quick sigh and then made a face and shook his head as if he was annoyed at himself for taking pity on himself. "You injured yourself. You were never supposed to injure yourself. You were supposed to stop those caped men today with your extraordinary ability by killing them and you failed even at that. You were supposed to fully realize your powers on the scouting, that's why I made a point to send you! You see, you don't listen to your instincts." Ringwaldr started pacing at this time. It seemed as if he really was baffled by Echo. The unbearable man was broken, confused, and infuriated that she had done this to him. Echo revelled in it a bit as he seemed tested and he continued in his mad ramblings. "This is why I didn't want to tell you or your father what I saw of you because I knew you would choke on the pressure you foolish girl!" As he said the last part he scoffed at her and Echo turned red in the face as she clenched her teeth. Before she could swing at him the door of his cell swung open and Asmund stood in the doorway blocking all light from coming through.

"Echo. Out. Now," Asmund demanded and Echo didn't have to be told twice. She angrily walked out of the room feeling ashamed and foolish for ever going there in the first place. What answers could he even give her? What good was he as a seer if he couldn't keep up with her ever-changing mind? It was him who was wrong.

There wasn't anything wrong with her.

Was there?

12
The Blind
Seer

The stranger that sat at the stronghold table had a bandage around his arm that was completely soaked with blood. After he had adjusted the bandage, he stared back at Echo with malice. She was, after all, the one who had given him the large wound.

Once her father had shooed Echo out of Ringwaldr's cell, he told her she was to sit in on interrogations. Echo could tell her father was unravelling at the seams and needed all the help he could get. It had indeed been a long day for everyone in the leading family. Now they were here, exhausted, wounded, and still working.

Echo stood beside her father with her arms crossed staring back at the man who had in turn given her a nasty purple bruise around her neck. Even though Echo's injury seemed to pale in comparison, they were both just as hateful towards one another. This man's pale skin reminded her of the redheaded stranger, and his light brown hair, though matted and messy, was a foreign shade to her as well. Echo hadn't noticed before but he was fairly young. He couldn't have been much older than her brother Kaapo. While Echo was lost in her thoughts, Asmund had already asked him several questions in what he presumed to be the man's native tongue but the intruder wasn't compliant. He seemed bored even.

After what felt like an hour, her father said another few words in the old Iivona language that Echo did not understand. Suddenly the intruder's fixed expression changed to confusion. There was an exchange between the two that seemed to startle her father. Standing behind Asmund was Kaapo and Takoda. Rythyn was guarding the door. Everyone in the room moved in a step closer at the sudden progress.

With clenched teeth Asmund stared blankly at the man but addressed his wife.

"Apparently, they haven't gotten any of our messengers. As far as they know, they've only received a threat over three weeks ago."

"Well that's just insane. We have sent several messengers."

"One I witnessed while scouting," Echo chimed in disbelief.

"I sent them one even before the scouting," Takoda began again.

"No, dear, you didn't… Ringwaldr did," Asmund said through gritted teeth. Suddenly putting all the pieces together, it didn't take long for everyone else in the room to figure it out as well.

"Wonderful," Takoda shouted in exasperation. It was clear she blamed herself for never taking that responsibility into her own hands but they never had a reason to not trust Ringwaldr.

Until now.

Ringwaldr was trying to orchestrate this tension between the two tribes. Asmund stood and waved to Rythyn to put the intruder back into his cell. Rythyn did exactly as he was told and then went back to his post beside the stronghold's front door. Asmund paced back and forth in the room as his family exchanged looks with one another. No one dared to speak first when they knew Asmund had more to say.

"You must realize, I can't kill the man. He has saved our tribe from much danger, but for some inexplicable reason, he has chosen now to become a traitor," Asmund said out loud in frustration but it seemed like he was talking to himself more than the others around him.

"Then we banish him," Takoda said simply and Asmund winced slightly. It was clear he had thought of that but there was something holding him back.

"I was thinking that, yes, but…"

"Where do you think Avila stands in all of this?" Kaapo so interestingly remarked. He looked as if he was caught in a daze, and everyone looked at him with the same confusion.

"Do you think she helped him? I don't know what to think, she was kidnapped… but returned back safely…

she follows him around like a pet, I mean I realize it's mostly because he's her mentor but it's strange… and not to mention she wasn't with him this morning. Now that I think about it, I haven't seen her much lately. Usually, she's tied to his side with a leash." Echo couldn't believe she hadn't thought of Avila. Ringwaldr had been speaking to her when he told her about his vision in the morning. The way she had answered him in their back-and-forth made Echo think that maybe she was a little clueless to his plans. Maybe he only let her know as much as he wanted her to. Was she an accomplice? There was no way she didn't know what he was up to, unless she was just so blind to everything happening around her. The family exchanged looks once again and then Asmund looked to Rythyn.

"Rythyn, find the girl. We will question her next." Asmund nodded to the man and he followed instructions without question. Asmund looked at his family one by one.

"Do not make it apparent to her that we suspect anything," Asmund stated and sat back down in his seat. He ran his hands through his thick hair and sighed heavily as he rested his face in his hands. Takoda lovingly rubbed his shoulder and kissed him on the top of his head.

"We must not fall apart now. I know what this betrayal must feel like for you in particular, but you are strong, in more ways than one," Takoda whispered to him. Asmund trusted Ringwaldr more than himself sometimes. The man played such a big role in saving their tribe before. Why did he choose to betray them, now? After two years of undoubted loyalty? None of it made sense.

Shortly after, Rythyn came back through the front door holding Avila by the shoulder. He pulled out the chair that the intruder had previously been sitting in and held it out for her. As she slowly took a seat, she stared wide-eyed in confusion at everyone in the room.

"I heard something had happened, but I'm not quite sure I know what's happening right now," Avila said slowly looking from Asmund and then to everyone in the room.

"Where were you this morning?" Asmund asked her calmly. The question seemed to confuse her even more.

"You mean before sunrise? I was in my cabin. Ringwaldr... woke me to tell me of a vision." Avila's eyes quickly fell on Echo and then went back to Asmund. Echo felt like she was naked and put on display all of a sudden. So many eyes kept falling on her for reasons she had no idea of. This time she knew the reason, but she didn't want to reveal to anyone that she had sleepwalked to Ringwaldr's cabin earlier.

"What was the vision?" The calm in her father's voice impressed Echo. After all he'd been through today, he was somehow still holding it together. Avila's eyes fell on Echo again. The struggle she was having inwardly was becoming more evident by the second. Nervously, she looked around as if someone were going to jump her from behind and then took a deep breath and began speaking very quickly.

"He'd been having visions of Echo in a battle." The young woman gulped down and heaved a large sigh. "In the battle, Echo fights off quite a few soldiers with the ease of her ability… and he told me not to say anything because it would throw her off. He kept saying she has great potential, and I didn't want to get in the way of anything. I felt guilty though. I had told you, Asmund, I was going to tell you if I had a vision, but he told me to keep it to myself…he *is* my mentor." Avila inhaled as if a giant weight was lifted off of her shoulders, but still looked as if she were struggling. "I've been so conflicted in the past few weeks, and when I was taken… I just… I don't know who to trust anymore. Ringwaldr told me he was the only one *to* trust. But he didn't even warn me that I'd be taken! He told me that not telling *you* was for your family's own good. There are things he knows that I can barely fathom." The young woman lifted her knees to her chest and hid her face in them. It was obvious that she was feeling some kind of shame. With the way Echo had seen Ringwaldr treat her at times, it made her wonder how much she was being taken advantage of in that relationship.

"It's all right Avila. Thank you for your honesty," Asmund said as tenderly as he could, expertly holding back all of his rage somewhere no one could see.

"Go back to your cabin and get some sleep dear," Takoda said softly, then went over to her to gently lay a hand on her shoulder. Avila looked up at her with tears swelling in her eyes.

"What's going to happen now?" The tone in the

room was easy enough to discern.

"You will be told at the meeting later on," Takoda said before Asmund spoke. Asmund was going to be as truthful as possible until his wife chimed in and used a calmer approach. Reading the room, Rythyn then escorted Avila out of the stronghold and back to her cabin.

"Do you still want to hear from Ringwaldr?" Takoda asked as she looked her husband in his tired eyes.

"Do you think he'll really say anything else?" Asmund asked.

"No." Unexpectedly, Ringwaldr's voice was heard through the walls of his cell. The cell was at the end of a three-door hallway in the stronghold. It was not very close to where they were conversing, but the family suspected if he hadn't heard something by now, he may have had a vision of his own outcome anyway. The family looked to one another. Asmund shook his head disappointedly and stood.

"Perhaps I will talk with him alone. As unwilling as he is to speak now, he might want to tell me something later," Asmund said slowly, still unsure of what to do about this situation. When Ringwaldr didn't object from his cell this time Asmund looked to his children and sighed.

"You two have made me very proud in the past few days. I know I've always asked a lot of you, but it's nice to know I can trust you both with these kinds of responsibilities. Even you Kaapo." Asmund looked to his son and the young man scoffed.

THE FIRST ECHO

"That's a little unwarranted don't you think?" Neither his mother nor his sister agreed with him when he looked to them for support and he disappointedly shrugged and accepted his fate. With the amount of times he did something he was told not to do, he realized maybe that's what everyone was talking about.

"I'd like it if you would both go to the pit, as it is close to noon. Let everyone know a decision is still being made and I will address everyone's questions tonight after the funeral. Relieve all forest duties, and be as honest as you can. Do not lie to your people. Make sure if they need anything, that you let them know you are available to them." The siblings nodded and left the cabin immediately.

The sun outside was bright and the sky was completely clear. The strangest thing about the day was that Echo couldn't hear the usual noise of birds chirping. After the chaos and blood curdling scream, it seemed all the birds in the area were hiding from this place in particular.

"Do you believe her?" Kaapo asked, pulling Echo out of her daze as she was squinting up at the sky.

"I don't see why I wouldn't. Even with how strong willed she seems Ringwaldr is terrible, and manipulative... he could easily over power her." Even with Echo's rambling Kaapo seemed to be lost in his thoughts.

"I guess you have a point. She seemed pretty out of it." Echo patted Kaapo's shoulder and they both started walking towards the pit. It was the place where everyone met for bonfires at night. Looking at it from the path, it seemed like the whole tribe was already there. Echo's breathing quickened. It was a little frightening to have a group of people that size look up to you when you didn't have a clue what you were doing. With how good he was at speaking in front of others Kaapo took the lead and jumped up on the nearest bench in the middle of the crowd of his people.

"Thank you for meeting with us. As of right now, my parents are making several decisions. We have found out that the intruders are under the impression that we have threatened them with war when we haven't, but we are going to work tirelessly to fix this." When Kaapo said it, he could see people in the crowd turn to each other in distress. He raised his voice as a low chatter began.

"This evening we will meet again for a funeral for our fallen tribesman, Sturla." Kaapo sighed and shook his head in disappointment, still in disbelief at the words that had left his mouth. "Anyone who was planning on being in the forest today for any duties has been relieved of them. My father wants no one out there at this time. We will stay alert and together. Even though they have left, that doesn't mean they're not waiting for us out there, to catch us off guard. Echo and I can help with anything you need, but don't expect us to answer any questions. We don't have very many answers right now." Kaapo jumped off the bench when he was finished and was easily swallowed by the crowd. Only half listening, Echo quickly hid from the questions as she was smaller and knew how to be invisible in crowds. She looked around specifically for Hanuel, and when she spotted his mother with a worried look, she manoeuvred through the crowd without detection.

"Xerxa! Where's Hanuel?" Xerxa looked surprised to see the girl and gave her a hug. The quick embrace, although alarming, relieved Echo to know Xerxa was still alive and unharmed.

"What did they do to you dear?" She carefully lifted Echo's Chin, inspecting the giant purple bruise on her neck. Echo gently grabbed onto her wrist and smiled with sad eyes. She was such a caring person, it made Echo extremely happy to know she wasn't hurt by the intruders.

"I'll be fine, but I know Hanuel was helping with Sturla. Have you seen him since?" Xerxa nodded sadly as she was reminded of the boy's death.

"When he was finished he came home and went to his room. He told me what happened. I can't believe I wasn't alert for any of it! And what they did to his face!" Echo nodded and gave her a quick hug again to reassure her that it was all right. Then she headed off for Hanuel's, jogging as fast as her pained leg would let her. It was either getting better, or she was becoming numb to the constant pain.

"Hanuel let me in!" she shouted through the front door. It only took her five quick pounds at the door before he swung it open quickly. His eyes were red and looked sore. His lip, even though cleaned of blood, Echo could now see the terrible gash he'd been left with. There was a bruise that had gone completely purple on his jaw and seeing him like this made Echo crash into his arms. He pulled her into the cabin and closed the door. Without hesitation he kissed her, but quickly winced in pain when he remembered his lip was torn.

"I'm so sorry!" Echo whispered and Hanuel laughed lightly at her worry.

"Not as sorry as I am." He shook his head and just held her close to him for a moment. Echo felt calmer with her head on his chest. He sighed heavily and she furrowed her brow.

"Are you all right?"

"No… it's all my fault he's dead."

Aghast Echo took his face in both of her hands, and even though he couldn't look her in the eyes she tried lifting his face so that he'd have to.

"What are you talking about? None of this is your fault." In disbelief she grabbed his hand and pulled him over to sit together at the table closest to them. She held both of his hands in hers. "Why would you ever think any of this is your fault Hanuel?"

Hanuel looked everywhere but at her before he answered.

"If I had just woken up earlier… I would've noticed you were gone. I would've been in the forest already. I could've helped them. I even heard the attackers and I just couldn't place it! I kept thinking to myself, when the intruders broke through the forest line, I would've already been there if I had just woken up earlier!" he rambled on, a pain in his voice as he continued. Echo's breath caught in her throat and she jolted out of her seat and stood there staring at him, frightened.

Your precious Hanuel would have been the one to cry over!

Her mouth went dry and she could have sworn that her heart skipped a beat. She was at a loss for words. She didn't even know how to comfort him after what he'd said. Ringwaldr knew Hanuel would have been dead if he had said anything to Echo. The timing was all off, and he had known it. She didn't know whether to hate Ringwaldr or reward him for saving Hanuel's life. Someone ended up dead, though, and there had to be a way where no one had. Hanuel looked confusedly up at her as she stood there caught in her wild thoughts.

"Echo?" he said softly. Slowly Echo's eyes came back into focus on Hanuel, and she sat back down in front of him. She gently ran a hand through his hair, moving it away from his eyes as he closed them, revelling in her comforting touch.

"Please don't blame yourself Hanuel... it's not your fault." Echo whispered. Hanuel didn't know how to answer her. He sighed and took the hand she ran through his hair in his. As Echo's mind raced, Hanuel led Echo to his room, and pulled her to him to lie on his cot. Quietly, they lay together, intertwined, as Echo mindlessly ran a hand through his curls again.

Even though she was trying to be there for him, her mind was elsewhere. She was feverishly trying to figure out outcomes in her head. Like a seer with no visions, she was trying to figure out why Ringwaldr made the choices he made. How far ahead was he? Was she truly someone who could keep him on his toes, or did he just say that to keep her in her place as his plans unfolded?

The energy around the evening's bonfire was silently sombre. The entire tribe had come to the fire fully draped in black robes. Most everyone had black robes made of dyed buckskins, but the elders of the Hemeran tribe wore robes made of crow feathers. They were very intricate robes made only for the dead's passing. The mother of the deceased had four other tribeswomen surrounding her at all times. Out of the four women none of them ever let go of the mother's hand or shoulder unless she had to wipe the tears on her face away. Sturla's father carried his son's body on a cot with the help of Manson, Jillik, and Hanuel. Everyone followed the young man's body in a slow procession to the lake. The only noise that could be heard were the many footsteps heading to the water's edge. There wasn't a soul who dared speak during this ritual. It was for the dead, and the dead were silent.

When they got to the water's edge, the cot was placed in the water carefully. The boy had been covered in flowers from head to toe by all of his tribe members wishing him well in the next life. The only part anyone could see of him was his face. In an eternal peace he slept as the four men that carried him pushed him adrift from shore. Asmund handed his father a bow and arrow that he had lit. Sturla's father reluctantly aimed and fired, letting out a groan of pain as he did so. The young man's mother sobbed loudly as the body went up in flames and the group silently walked back to the fire as one.

A feast began, and even though no one really wanted to talk, chatter started up. They began to tell stories about the boy around the fire. There were bursts of laughter, quickly followed by sad expressions. The memories that they had with Sturla were all they had now, and it seemed unfair. He was too young, too vibrant, too loyal to his tribe. He didn't deserve this.

On a log fairly close to the bonfire, Echo sat, squeezing Hanuel's hand a little too tightly and making him worry. He wrapped an arm around her shoulders, and Echo leaned into him for a moment until she noticed her father across the way talking to the Sutrla's parents. Her many thoughts of Ringwaldr knowing that Sturla or Hanuel would die made her crazy. She had to tell her father. Once she noticed her father had finished speaking with Sturla's parents, Echo shot up from her seat. Without any warning, she jogged over to her father saying a very quick sorry to Hanuel who was confused by the sudden change of pace. He followed behind her as she rushed over to her father.

"He knew. He knew that Sturla was going to die and he just let him die. When I spoke to him in the cell. He knew! This is all his fault!" Asmund looked slightly confused at his daughter. He rested both of his hands on her shoulders pulling her off to the side where they could talk more quietly, and he could try to calm her down.

"Echo? What are you talking about?"

"Ringwaldr. He knew Sturla was going to die and he just let him. He told me in his cell, that if he had told me about his vision I would have screwed it up and…" Echo looked to Hanuel who looked just as confused as her father, and she wished he hadn't followed her over. "He said… Hanuel would be the one to cry over right now, if he had told me about his vision. But I don't believe him! If he knew, why wouldn't he have seen a way to save them both!"

"Echo. Go home. Get some rest. Thank you for telling me this," Asmund said calmly and pulled him to her for a hug. When her father left, Echo looked to Hanuel who was staring at her with a look of disbelief and horror. She reached for his hand but he backed away and ran to his cabin. She followed hastily behind him.

13

"Why didn't you tell me?"

"Hanuel, I was trying to figure it out in my head, I thought he was just lying to me to anger me!"

"You still should have told me, Echo. I blamed myself, and I wasn't wrong!"

"No Hanuel! It wasn't your fault! And there was no time to even tell you! There were more important things, like you were helping with Sturla, and I just didn't want to upset you more."

"I'm upset *now*!"

"Haneul I'm sorry. Please, can we just... can we just lay down and... forget about everything that's going on?"

"My friend is dead, and now I find out it was me or him. Yeah, let me just sleep it off," he retorted sardonically, brushing off Echo's bad idea with a wave of his hand.

"You know that's not how I meant it…" Echo mumbled after what he said had made her wince. She was sitting on his bed and he was pacing back and forth in his room. His parents were still at the bonfire, but they would be home soon as it was getting darker much faster now. The two had gotten into the cabin and immediately started bickering. It was a back and forth that wasn't getting any better. There was a lantern in the corner of the room that flickered wildly when they were talking to each other. Right now, in the dense silence, it was still and unwavering. Echo stared at the flame, as Hanuel continued to pace. She was feverishly trying to figure out some way to console him. The still flame her eyes focused on was relaxing to look at as a storm went on inside her mind.

"I need to be alone." Looking up at him, Echo sighed, exasperated by the words. Hanuel had come to a complete halt to look at her. Echo was sure there was disgust behind his eyes and she felt ashamed. It made Echo's heart hurt.

"Hanuel please! I don't want you to be alone right now. You can be mad at me all you want, but you need to know it wasn't your fault."

"Echo!" Hanuel shouted and she winced at his anger once again. This was all too hard. She held back tears but stood up to get right in his face.

"I'm not leaving you alone until I know that you don't think it's your fault." Hanuel rolled his eyes and shook his head at her stubbornness. Saddened, he slowly took a seat on the bed where she had just been sitting. Burying his face into his hands, he continued.

"Echo I'll talk to you in the morning, please, just... let me be right now. If what you told me he said is true..." Pausing for a moment and taking his face out of his hands he looked like he was in shock. "I could've died today. I could've been that body on the lake, but I also could have saved a friend and now I just feel so guilty and thankful all at once." Hanuel grimaced, disgusted with himself that he could ever be thankful that someone died in his place. Echo's eyes swelled up and she got on her knees and held on to his wrists with both of her hands so he had to look her in the face. The sudden change in character was so startling to him because she'd never done it before. He was used to her being stone cold and persistent. She was trembling.

"Can't you see that's why I don't want to leave you right now? Remember when you said you didn't know what to do if you could never hear my breathing again? Well I had that moment today and now I can't imagine leaving you because something is telling me I might never see you again! You can be mad at me, you can push me away all you want. I'll sit in the corner and sob if I have to, but I'm not leaving!"

Hanuel sighed. His face softened at the words. She was almost delirious. It seemed to be making sense to him now.

"Okay, okay... just calm down." Frustrated, he paused to ease his tone. "I'm just angry. I don't know whether to feel relieved or sad." Echo wasn't holding on to his wrists tightly, so he just took them back from her. Gently, he grabbed Echo by her wrists and pulled her up to get her to sit beside him. Looking over at her his eyes scanned the large bruise around her neck. It made him gulp down hard.

"I'm sorry I didn't tell you when he said it. I thought he was trying to confuse me. Then when you told me how you would have been there if you were only minutes earlier... it could have really happened! It could've been you. I feel so terrible." Echo closed her eyes hard. At that moment she saw Sturla's smiling face and her eyes began to swell up, "it feels like Ringwaldr has all the answers to help everyone, but for some sick reason, he's choosing to keep them to himself! It's maddening!" Hanuel listened, as he always did when Echo rambled on, and then reached out for her neck, gently touching the bruised skin. She didn't back away. It didn't hurt as he wasn't really putting pressure on it. Hanuel silently forgave her as she explained herself and then his eyes went from her bruise to her eyes.

"You know I tried to get to you before he jumped on you. That's when the other one hit me in the mouth. I think I would've killed him if I got to him Echo. I don't know how you didn't."

"I... thought about it... I had the knife ready, I saw myself doing it in my mind." Echo gulped down hard as the thought came back to her and continued. "But I stopped because I've never done that before... and I didn't want to be that person. The one Ringwaldr sees... he said I was supposed to kill ten of those men... I overheard him when I... sleepwalked there this morning. I was so scared I was going to and what good would that have done? It still wouldn't have saved Sturla. There would be blood on my hands... I'm thankful I didn't... I would have been giving Ringwaldr what he wants."

Hanuel sighed deeply, rubbing his forehead. It looked like he wanted to speak but was so exasperated he gave up and decided to lay back on his bed. He didn't have any energy left to respond. Today's events were becoming too much and Echo was just glad he didn't want to kick her out anymore. She sat at the end of his bed and brought her knees to her chest, resting her head on one of them.

"I want to forget about everything that's going on now," Hanuel said softly as he curled up on his side still facing her. Cautiously, Echo lay in front of him. When she was comfortable and he didn't seem to detest it, she ran a hand through his hair. He let out a tense breath and closed his eyes.

"If I could pick all the bad memories out of your hair I would," Echo said softly. Even with his sad expression Hanuel smirked ever so slightly.

"With these curls? You'd be here for ages... you should get started now."

"I said *if*." Echo teased and Hanuel pulled her closer to him to wrap his arms around her waist. In turn, she wrapped her arms around his neck and held his head to her chest. She continued to run a hand through his hair as he slowly fell asleep in her arms. Echo noticed herself listening to his breathing as he fell asleep. It became deeper and slow, a soothing sound that was as comforting as a bedtime story. There weren't enough words to express how grateful she was that she could still lie with him like this. The very idea that he had been the dead body found kept coming back to her in the night, waking her from the light sleep she would fall out of. Every time she awoke from the tiny nightmare, she would give him a gentle squeeze in her arms to know he was still there.

"Echo!"

All through the night, she did not get a lot of sleep. When she heard a rapping at the front door and her brother calling her name she was the first to get up, startling Xerxa who was groggily walking over to open the door. Echo awkwardly said hello, and let Xerxa know that she could get it for her, already knowing it was her brother, Kaapo.

"You know, if you're gonna do this whole, sleeping with each other thing, you need to pick a consistent place where we can find you because this is the second day in a row that it's been difficult." Echo's face went red when Kaapo started in on her because Xerxa was still within earshot. She could tell he was annoyed.

"What do you want? It's sunrise," Echo asked him

impatiently.

"*Oh*? Oh is it?" Kaapo began in feigned shock. He put his hand over his eyes, squinting, to take a better look at the sunrise then looked back to her. "Wow, I thought it was the other one, I thought it was *sunset*, so now I'm here at the wrong time, and I'll just go." All through his little charade, Echo stared at him deadpan. She was much too tired to be finding his antics very funny.

"Would you just... explain yourself?" Echo crossed her arms over her chest and her brother shrugged.

"Mom came to get me, and told me to find you and come to the soldier's stronghold. They're going to tell everyone about their decision at breakfast." Kaapo waited for her response and Echo sighed.

"Okay, let me just tell Hanuel so he doesn't wake up to me gone for the second time in two days." Kaapo rolled his eyes and Echo went back into Hanuel's room. It was a wonder how he was such a heavy sleeper with that really good hearing of his, but maybe it was a blessing for him to be able to shut it off when he slept.

"Hanuel?" Echo said softly as she sat on the side of his cot and gently moved his hair behind his ear. When he didn't stir she leaned in closer to his ear and then said his name again at a regular speaking volume. The young man jumped and his eyes shot tiredly open.

"Oh, you're still here... I didn't have to go looking for you," Hanuel said quietly in a relieved tone.

"Yeah, I thought I'd make it easier for you this morning." Echo grinned and he smirked back at her.

"I've got to go. My parents need me and Kaapo. I'll see you at the pit. We're supposedly making an announcement." Echo leaned in and kissed his cheek, but he frowned and pulled her in again to kiss her lips. He winced as he remembered his cut but then smiled up at her. The notion made her swoon just a bit, and she immediately stood and cleared her throat. She could see the disappointment on Hanuel's face but she had to go. Even though he proved to be a beautiful getaway from her regular responsibilities, they would catch up to her at some point.

When she got outside, Kaapo had his arms crossed over his chest as he leaned on a post that held up the patio's canopy. He stared at her with a brow raised and she looked at him like he had two heads.

"Why on earth are you looking at me like that for?"

"No reason, its nothing," he said slowly. His expression seemed condescending.

"That doesn't sound like nothing."

"It's nothing." Knowing he was irritating his sister without much effort, Kaapo smirked. Echo scoffed at him and rolled her eyes.

"Fine then, let's go," Echo breathed, exasperated with her brother as usual. The two refrained from speaking to each other, even with how much Kaapo liked to bug Echo, they both seemed to be lost in their thoughts with what could happen today. Echo was almost certain Ringwaldr would be banished, but then what would happen to Avila? She had saved Echo's life at least once. Echo felt like she had a debt to repay, and it wouldn't be repaid if the woman was kicked out of Hemera. The intruders were a whole other problem. How did her father plan to bring them back to Iivona? Or what did he plan to do with them at all? So many questions made Echo sick to her stomach with nerves.

When they finally entered the soldiers' stronghold Echo felt like two days had gone by with how many thoughts went through her mind. Her father and mother were standing, talking softly to Rythyn and two younger soldiers. When the five people in the room noticed the siblings enter, Rythyn nodded to Asmund and directed the two young men down the hall to a cell.

"Morning, my loves," Takoda said softly and went over to kiss Echo on her forehead and then hug Kaapo. "As we all suspected we have decided to banish him. We will announce it this morning at the fire. We've already sent a messenger to everyone's cabin telling them we will have a meeting."

"And what of Avila?" Kaapo asked with a furrowed brow.

"Avila may do as she wishes. But whether she chooses to stay or go your father and I will keep a close eye on her. We ask that you do as well."

Kaapo and Echo gave each other a confused look. Even though the girl seemed burdened by Ringwaldr she might change her mind and go with him. The idea of it made Echo wary.

"And the intruders? What will happen next?" Echo asked, looking to her father.

"I'm bringing them back to Iivona myself and having

a discussion with their leader if they give me the chance. We're travelling to the border at sunrise tomorrow, with a horse and cart of prisoners. It should take four days and three nights to arrive as safely as possible. That is if everything runs smoothly. I will be asking you two to stay here and tend to our people. Because we are unsure of any other attack right now, we're going to have to double the number of scouts on watch at night and in the day. I'm leaving you two in charge of that." Echo and Kaapo shared a look again, this time they both seemed more nervous than before.

"All right, it's time," Takoda commented as she noticed Rythyn come down the hall holding Ringwaldr by the arm. It was as if a wave of malice wafted into the room like smoke, and everyone who was hit by it began to glare over at the man. Unsurprisingly he kept the same cool expression on his face. Echo was well aware he already knew what was in store for him.

The leading family walked together to the pit in an uncomfortable silence. Ringwaldr's hands were tied behind his back and he was being led by Rythyn and another soldier on each side of him. The crowd seemed to open up as they all arrived, and Asmund, Rythyn, and Ringwaldr all stood next to the bench Kaapo had stood on earlier to make his announcement in the centre of the crowd. The fire in the pit was small and popped gently as the three silently took their places. The crowd was so quiet no one dared to even breathe heavily as they waited for Asmund's words. Looking at Ringwaldr's face, Echo noticed his expression suddenly change, if only for a moment. He was smirking, and then went back to his concealed look. The moment made a chill run down her spine.

"Hemera, today we will banish Ringwaldr for knowingly letting an attack happen on this tribe that resulted in the death of Sturla. This man actively stopped messages from our camp to Iivona's tribe which caused the kidnapping a few days ago, and of course, this very brutal attack today."

"Kill him!"

Echo looked out to the crowd, startled at the voice, but understood a bit more when she noticed it was Sturla's father who had shouted it out. Only a few other members agreed when they heard it but Asmund held both his hands up to calm the crowd.

"It has been decided... that because he has saved our tribe before, we will not take his life willingly." Half of the crowd seemed to revolt, and the other half were unsure of how to act.

"But," Ringwaldr chimed in his monotone voice as he rolled his eyes. Asmund looked confusedly to him but then continued when Rythyn shook the man to get him to be silent.

"But, if Ringwaldr is to show his face amongst the trees of our settlement, he will be killed on sight, and that is an instruction for anyone if you see him. You have the right to kill him or tell a soldier." Asmund looked to Ringwaldr who had a steady gaze set to the back of the crowd where Avila stood. Echo followed his gaze and looked over at the woman who seemed to be extremely bewildered by the situation.

"Tomorrow, Takoda and I will begin our travel to Iivona to try and mend what is happening. In the meantime, scouts will be stationed at every point of the forest's edge. Any hunting that must be done in the sacred forest will be done in a single group, and my children will be your active leaders. Come to them for anything you may need." Asmund turned to Ringwaldr, "As for you..." Ringwaldr's gaze never left Avila's bewildered face. "You will be escorted out. Now." Before anyone could move Ringwaldr decided it was his turn to speak. His voice boomed like Asmund's.

"I'd rather walk myself out but thankyou Asmund, for that *lovely* speech." Ringwaldr looked to Asmund with that expressionless face, and then set his sights to the crowd. "Foresight, is not for the faint of heart. The things I've seen would invoke an insanity inside of you that you could not control." Even though he was set in his emotionless gaze on the crowd, Echo could hear the anger behind his words. Then he looked at her directly in the crowd. Echo, whose stomach turned at the eye contact, gulped down. Ringwaldr continued. "And Echo, because I *thoroughly* enjoy all of our conversations... come find me when you want more answers... darling," he said with a smirk. He only ever seemed to show emotion to her, and when he did it made her so uncomfortable.

In the next moment.

THE FIRST ECHO

Just a blink of an eye.

Ringwaldr disappeared from existence.

The ropes that held his arms back disappeared with him as well and a black cloud of hazy smoke was left where he last was.

A shriek from the back of the crowd let everyone know that Avila was furious. She pushed to the front and was wildly looking around in every direction. Everyone was still in shock. They didn't understand how he had been there one moment and gone the next.

Breath caught in Echo's throat and she felt dizzy. The world around her seemed to shift and she grabbed onto Kaapo's arm as she felt like she was about to faint. Kaapo grabbed onto her and shook her out of her daze. Echo finally started to breathe again and looked at her father.

"Ringwaldr?" Asmund bellowed, looking around the crowd, furious with the events unfolding. "Find him!" He pointed to several soldiers that had walked down with them from the stronghold but Takoda pointed to Jillik in the crowd.

"Everyone stay put! Jillik!" Takoda had already thought quickly enough to realize he'd be their best way to know if Ringwaldr's feet touched the ground. The young man nodded and even as he was still stunned he got to the ground and a few seconds later disappointedly got to his feet again. He had sensed no running footsteps. Asmund pointed to his soldiers again.

"Search the edge. Make sure you protect our

grounds. I don't know what he is capable of!"

Echo stood there stunned. She wasn't the first of her kind. Ringwaldr knew that, but played into it so masterfully. Jillik couldn't sense what didn't touch the ground. Ringwaldr was echoing, and apparently he had much more control over it than Echo did.

Hanuel came running over to her and Kaapo wide-eyed.

"I can't even hear running. How did he get so far? You've never gotten that far before have you?" the young man asked as he looked at Echo. She gulped down. That wasn't completely true. The tree that she had echoed from the first time she'd ever done it was much higher than the short distance she had covered before. Was there no limit to distance? If she controlled it better, could she disappear to wherever he disappeared to? There was no way of knowing now, but she had so many questions that he knew he was the only one who could answer all of them. Here she was, just a pawn in his game. It seemed like the perfect time to faint, and with that, Echo did.

"Well, I think I've had about enough of her sleeping through her problems." The voice seemed muffled and far away. There was too much light in the room for Echo to open her eyes comfortably, and when she hadn't, she was doused in a bucket of lukewarm water as punishment.

Sputtering for air she sat up right in what felt like the cot in Eira's cabin and she groaned. When her eyes fully opened and were seeing clearly after the unsuspecting bath, she looked to everyone in the room. Eira sat at the edge of the bed with a bored expression. Kaapo was sitting to her right and trying to hold back a laugh. Hanuel was sitting on the opposite side of them both with a grimace.

"Why is that the second time in one week I've been woken up by water?"

"I asked her not to," Hanuel answered anxiously.

"I got her the water," Kaapo added calmly.

"Oh come now, it was one bucket. You wouldn't have drowned." Eira huffed and rolled her eyes as she dragged her feet to the other side of the room where she placed the bucket on her working table.

"Did you get any sleep last night Echo? Did you not eat anything? Both of those things together, added to the fright we all witnessed are a good mix for a fainting spell," Eira said. Echo didn't answer as she was right in all of those things. She hadn't slept well, she hardly ate or drank anything because of the chaos of the day and night yesterday, and she suddenly realized Ringwaldr disappearing wasn't a hallucination.

Everyone had seen it.

"So... that really happened then? He echoed? He can do what I can do, but he's obviously been doing it longer if it was that easy for him." She heaved a heavy sigh and looked to Hanuel who seemed as disappointed as she was.

"I've written it in my compendium, for anyone wondering... you know what's strange? I never thought of foresight to be connected to a Hirzla. I just thought it was an ability one of the creatures had, but we couldn't place because it isn't like we can speak to them. It makes a lot of sense, though. Suspicious creatures those things are. I assume that's what makes them so deceptive. Seeing... and then gone in the blink of an eye. Seeing and blinking? Blinking and seeing? What a funny use of words." Eira rambled on as she was reaching for her compendium on her shelf, and the three teenagers exchanged looks. The crazy old woman might have been onto something.

"Did they leave for Iivona already?" Echo turned to Kaapo and he nodded.

"They came in to check on you while you were passed out. Hanuel brought you here when you fainted," Kaapo answered.

"Aren't you getting tired of carrying me?" Echo looked over at Hanuel, feeling a bit guilty.

"What a strange way to say thank you," Hanuel said in a feigned confusion then smirked at her and Echo grinned back at him.

Kaapo rolled his eyes at the two, and stood up to help Eira grab the compendium that she kept putting on a shelf much too high for her.

"So, the compendium now has Ringwaldr under Hirzla? He's a seer and echoer? That doesn't sound right anymore, since you're not the only one who can do it." Kaapo added as he looked over at his sister. "I liked

Eira's word for it, blinking. So now we know that he can see… and blink." Kaapo began slowly, shaking his head at the ridiculous sentence that had just left his mouth.

"It's better if we call it blinking, I don't want to name something after me that I have in common with that man." Echo sighed.

"Yes well, I don't understand why his smoke is black. You've described Echo's as green. I saw it in her wound," Eira started as she looked to Hanuel who confirmed with a nod. "In my experience, Hirzla's bones and antlers usually give that off, so it makes sense, I've established that much… why would his be black?" Echo looked over at her, for as blind as the woman was sometimes, she sure was perceptive. The three sat caught in their thoughts for a moment. Then Echo suddenly remembered she had seen the Hirzla in the forest. It wasn't entirely off-topic, but because of the attack, she was never able to tell anyone after it happened.

"I saw it! I saw the stag," the words left her mouth the same way she had spit out the water that woke her up. "The antler was broken. Sorry, I know we're trying to figure out why his smoke is different, but I had to tell you before I forgot. This morning I dead walked to Ringwaldr's cab—"

"What?" Eira interrupted.

"Just listen," Echo insisted, "I overheard him speaking to Avila about how I was supposed to kill a bunch of intruders. That's when I ran away because I was scared something was going to overtake me and make me do what he described." Echo gulped down and looked at everyone who was now staring at her intently, "I had a choice; to stay out in the forest and ignore the signs or follow the stag's green haze."

"Did the thing ask you to follow it?" asked Kaapo, his sarcastic tone made Echo shoot a glare in his direction.

"The stag led me to the Iivona camp in the woods, Kaapo. It's why I ran back from the forest." Everyone stared at Echo with nothing to say. It was a lot of information to take in and process.

"What's going on?" The voice was groggy and seemed to be in pain. Echo had just realized that the young man who was guarding the border with Sturla the other day, Daes, was still in the room. Beaten and bruised, but not bloodied anymore as he'd obviously been cleaned up by Eira as soon as he came in.

"Don't worry yourself Daes. Get some rest, it will get a lot quieter in here once I kick these rowdy three out," Eira said going over to the young man's bed and fixing his sheets over him. Disregarding Eira's comment Kaapo walked over to the boy's side looking him over from head to toe.

"How are you feeling, friend?" he asked him and Daes shrugged. You could see the sudden sense of guilt wash over him.

"It hurts a lot, but it could've been worse from what I was told when I woke up. I feel terrible… I tried to stop them. Sturla tried so hard to warn everyone. I gave up after a few hits," he said shaking his head holding back tears and looking down at his hands.

"That doesn't look like a few," Hanuel said in disbelief. "You did all you could. We all did... don't blame yourself," Hanuel said slowly, flashing Echo a look. She sighed in relief, glad that he had finally come to that conclusion. She reached for his hand and held it. He squeezed hers back.

"All right. You three, out. This one needs sleep and you shouldn't be waking him. You're all fine you've been here much too long!" Eira ranted.

"I feel so loved and cared for when I'm here," Kaapo commented sarcastically as he was being pushed out the front door by the old woman. The three said a short goodbye to Daes as they left.

Once out of the cabin they all seemed to have the same feeling of being there twelve too many times. Looking up at the sky Echo realized it was just a little after noon. The sun was still high and she had to squint up at it.

"Well boys... what now?" She looked from one to the other and Kaapo shrugged tiredly but then a sudden burst of energy hit him and he looked to her wide-eyed.

"I say we train you up. Get you as good as black smoke, just in case he decides to come back. I have a feeling he's a little mad about whatever his plan was falling through."

Echo stared wide-eyed at her brother. Even when he seemed insane he made good points.

"Do you think his plans really fell through? I mean I know our parents are now working tirelessly to fix the relationship between Iivona but... are we sure this isn't what he wanted?" Hanuel scrunched up his face in confusion after her question, then shook his head.

"Echo, you even said yourself that you didn't kill ten men like his vision. You didn't feed into what he wanted. He is banished and could possibly be killed if he comes back. That doesn't seem like something he'd set out to do."

"Yes, but he has a way of... getting what he wants." Echo started and then stopped herself. If she took herself down this path of infinite possibilities she didn't know if she'd get out of the vicious cycle. "Nevermind, I don't want to think about him for a while... I'm ready to be trained up. We can't go to the falls though. We should be staying out of the forest, and if people need to find us for anything while our parents are gone..."

"Soldier's training yard, I got someone who I want to train you up. It's a wide open space. People will see us if they need us." Kaapo had already decided and Echo shrugged.

"Okay, I guess... Hanuel, you'll join us, right?"

"I'll follow you anywhere remember?" Without hesitation the boy answered her and she grinned up at him. She jumped on his back so he'd carry her and Kaapo gagged.

"If you're going to be gross in front of me, we're going to have to come up with a limit, and this boy must be tired of carrying you. Have you just forgotten how to use your feet now that you can *blink* places?" Kaapo started and Hanuel laughed while Echo glared over at him.

THE FIRST ECHO

The three teenagers went off to the soldier's yard, letting a fellow messenger know on their way there to tell all the tribe's people that if they needed anything, they'd be there until it was time for the night's bonfire.

EPILOGUE

Two years before

The night was cold and damp. The rain hadn't stopped since noon, and now Ringwaldr and Avila were soaked to the bone. Avila kept her anger towards Mother Nature to herself as the two trudged on through the night. They had attempted to light torches, but when they realized they would not stay lit in this downpour, they continued walking through the cloud of darkness that overtook the sacred forest. After hours of trekking tirelessly through the mud, Avila had finally had enough.

"Where are we? How much further? This trail used to be clear of debris," she snarled. Ringwaldr shook his head at her petulance.

"You haven't been here since you were a child. What would you know of this path now?" Ringwaldr stated under his breath.

"I remember it was much shorter for one!" she shot back.

"Settle down. We're close. Everything I saw in my vision is becoming clearer."

"That's nice, but I still don't see any cabins or people and—"

Immediately Ringwaldr and Avila went silent, frozen still in place. There were now two spears pointed directly at their faces. Two muscular men in dark green buckskin capes looked curiously from Ringwaldr to Avila. The dark clouded the features of their faces, but Ringwaldr could sense their uncertainty when they didn't immediately move to kill him and Avila. He was sure that only one of the two strangers could see himself and Avila as well as a bloodhound right now.

"Before you kill us! I have a message for Asmund." The two men exchanged a look of concern. Most intruders didn't ask for their tribe's leader by name. One of the men looked back at Ringwaldr,

"Where do you hail from?" asked the caped man furthest from Ringwaldr as he moved his spear closer to his neck. Ringwaldr stood unflinching. Why would a man fear death when he already knew his future?

"Our home is of little importance. We've come directly from the Deadlock Mountains, but that is not our ancestry." Ringwaldr answered the two scouts calmly. The caped men looked at each other again and eased up on their spears. One of them grabbed Ringwaldr's hands and placed them behind his back. The other scout tied Avila's hands behind her back. They led them both through the forest to a pathway of cabins. It was very dark, and the familiar path of Hemera had no torches that were lit. The rain and wind had proven too strong even to have flames under the shelter of a patio still burning. However, the candles lit within the cabins could be seen from outside and gave the entire settlement an eerie glow. The two foreigners were led to the leader's cabin and pushed into chairs at Asmund's family table in front of the leader who was in discussion with Rythyn and his wife at the time.

"What's this?" Asmund asked his two scouts, and before either could answer Ringwaldr interrupted them.

"I come to you from the Deadlock Mountains. Like I've told your men here, I do not hail from there. I am merely a traveller passing through. I've had a vision I must relay to you." Ringwaldr's emotionless face droned on, and Asmund looked just as bored.

In the next room, Kaapo, Echo, and Hanuel all jumped, startled by the noise of the front door opening. All night they had been playing a game in the siblings' room. Whenever they'd hear rolling thunder, the last one to yell the old rhyme, *No worse danger is more frightening than a force of nature,* had to submit to a dare by the first person who had said it. It wasn't unusual for Hanuel to stay overnight when his father had to discuss plans with Asmund. It was a regular occurrence of their childhood and the reason he was there now. The children were laughing at a dare they had just put Hanuel through when the unexpected sound of the door swinging open at this time of night startled them all into silence. Kaapo and Echo ran over to peer through the door.

Kaapo easily beat Echo there and took up most of the space. They spent a moment pushing each other around until Kaapo finally let her see too, and she placed her head underneath her brother's. When Hanuel noticed the two settle, he got in on the action and put his head underneath Echo's who got a mouthful of curls when he did so.

"You think you're a seer?" Asmund raised a brow as he said it. At the time, seers were not taken seriously. No one had mastered the craft in Asmund's tribe. One man had lost his mind trying, and another had two visions come to fruition and was never right again. *'Seers'* were not a reliable type; in all of Asmund's experiences, they were con artists. All of Hemera knew that seeing the future was not something any animal could do in the sacred forest. Therefore, the sacred forest would grace no human with that gift.

"I *am* a seer," Ringwaldr said, trying his best to keep his teeth unclenched.

"And how do you know about me? Why would I be so important as to be in your vision?" Asmund spoke slowly. His tone was condescending. He'd already been dealing with enough problems within his tribe. He wasn't in the mood for this charade.

"When I heard of you in Iivona, you were the man with the strength of a mountain bear. That's what caused it, I presume."

"Quite a long way to follow a vision of a man you do

not know."

"Correct. If that had been the *only* one, I would not subject myself to this mockery." Asmund raised a brow and smirked at the retort. Whether these two drenched strangers were telling the truth or not, Ringwaldr had now piqued Asmund's interest. It appeared self-loathing, and awareness was the only thing Ringwaldr had to display to catch the leader's attention.

"And your name, *seer*?"

The seer hesitated for a moment, but his emotionless stare never changed.

"Ringwaldr, and this is Avila. She is my student." Avila nodded to Asmund shortly as he looked to her.

"Ah… a student? That would imply you've mastered your skill." Asmund smirked again. As impressive as the two were, he still did not believe them. Ringwaldr could sense the tone and ignored it.

"The hunters that you send out at sunrise will encounter a feral mountain bear. A pack of bloodhounds will have killed her young, and she will not care. She will attack your men, and you will lose ten."

"Do all seers rhyme?" Asmund couldn't help but make the joke, and Rythyn snorted as he held back a laugh. Hanuel chuckled lightly as well and Echo shushed him before they got caught as his curls tickled the underside of her chin. Ringwaldr stopped and glared at both of the men for a moment but then continued when their teasing stopped.

"Your son needs to be on that hunt. He will shift—"

"What do you know of my son?" Asmund said lowly,

getting to his feet slowly now. As far as Asmund knew these two were strangers, and it was quite startling to know that Ringwaldr knew about his kin. The three children standing in the doorway went wide-eyed. Ringwaldr clenched his teeth. Being interrupted was something he loathed, and he wasn't intimidated by Asmund's sheer size. He stood up, matching him in stature but not height. When Ringwaldr arose the two scouts behind him took a step closer. Everyone in the room held their breath, ready for one of them to throw a fist.

"He will shift and save all ten of your men. It will be the first shift of many, and if he fails tomorrow at sunrise, he will not realize his full potential in time. Two years down the line, he will fall in battle if he is negligent tomorrow."

"You're insane. It would be in your best interest to leave my settlement now."

"Let us prove it to you," Avila chimed in. Her tone was much calmer than her counterpart's. She didn't want to stand, knowing there was no reason when her height, yet taller than the average woman, did not tower over anyone else in the room. "Let us stay until high noon tomorrow. Send your son out, or don't, but wouldn't the satisfaction of knowing now rather than later be better than waiting two years to be proven wrong with a body?" Avila stared at Asmund with a genuine look of concern. Asmund sighed with a smirk. Takoda who had seemed bored with the conversation since it had started suddenly sat up right in her chair.

The girl seemed to have a point. Asmund looked to his wife, who shrugged and waved her hand carelessly toward the two strangers.

"Fine. You will stay in a cell tonight. I don't know what you are capable of, and I'm not letting you near my people until I know you do not wish us harm." Asmund said after getting his wife's approval.

"May I make a request?" Ringwaldr asked.

"Oh, our guests need something more now?" Rythyn added tiredly. Ignoring the statement, Ringwaldr continued.

"May I speak to your boy?" Asmund thought for a moment and then looked over to one of the scouts.

"No… I will tell him he will hunt tomorrow, but in no way will you speak to him, or even know him for that matter unless your vision comes to fruition. I know how con artists like you work. You are not the first to come to me from another land promising more than you have." Ringwaldr smirked for a moment but then reverted to his emotionless state. The two glared at each other and then Asmund nodded to his scouts to take him away. The two were dragged out and as they left Avila looked worriedly to Ringwaldr.

"That didn't go as planned. You have to tell the boy what to do," she hissed, and the scout dragging her away shook her to be silent.

"Quiet Avila," Ringwaldr mumbled under his breath, "everything is going as planned." The two were dragged a short way to the soldiers' stronghold and thrown into a dark, damp cell. The bottom inch of the cell had flooded. Avila scoffed as her moccasins, though already wet, became flooded with water.

"How delightful, pulled out of the rain to be thrown into a pool." The scout that locked the door behind them snorted at the comment. Then he took post at the front door of the soldiers' stronghold out of sight. Avila sat down on the makeshift cot in the room and took off her moccasins, trying her hardest to squeeze any water she could get out of them.

"You didn't speak to the boy. How is he going to know what to do?"

"We don't have to speak to the boy. He just has to hear us, and I know one of them can." Avila looked confused at the words. Ringwaldr took a deep breath in.

"If the boy wants to stop the itching under his skin he must yell like he's never yelled before," Ringwaldr said loudly and then waited. Avila looked at him like he was crazy. When Ringwaldr hadn't heard the guard react, he sighed and took a deep breath. Avila sat on the cot, looking confusedly up at him as she smacked her shoe against the wall. Ringwaldr rolled his eyes and grabbed her wrist to hold it still for a moment.

"Tell the boy to yell like he's never yelled before, and he'll shift into the bear!" Ringwaldr shouted and then immediately heard footsteps on the other side of their cell door. Avila grabbed her shoe with her other hand and swatted at Ringwaldr's shoulder.

"Why are you yelling at me?" Avila snarled in a whisper.

"Quiet down!" With a few knocks, Toff, a scout who

could run at a rapid speed, proven by how quickly he got to the door, pounded on it. Avila rolled her eyes.

"What are you yelling for? They're not going to tell him anything!" Avila sighed and crossed her arms over her chest. Ringwaldr had disappointed her more than her wet shoes.

"The soldier's son can hear me. I know he can. He was in the room. He never leaves their side," Ringwaldr shot at her impatiently.

"Oh, *him*." Avila's eyes widened. She had remembered something Ringwaldr had told her before of the boy that wasn't all that pleasant.

"Yes," Ringwaldr answered her impatiently. "The one that always seems to take us all down the wrong path."

"And how are you so certain we're on the right path now?"

"We've been over this Avila. It's not simple, and I'm not repeating myself." Avila rolled her eyes. What a strange thing for a teacher to tell their student.

Back in the leader's cabin, the three teenagers were sitting on the floor in a small circle. Kaapo and Echo eagerly watched as Hanuel made strange faces, undoubtedly trying to shuffle through all the amplified sounds going on around him.

"I think I can hear them…" Hanuel spoke slowly, trying to concentrate.

"What are they saying? More stuff about me?"

Kaapo asked rather loudly and Echo shushed him.

"Give him a minute!" she whispered, swatting at her brother, and Kaapo sighed as he rolled his eyes.

If...s...it...in...he must yell...

"I don't know if I heard that right."

"Heard what Hanuel?" Echo asked softly.

"Itch? Skin? If? He must yell?" Hanuel said slowly, closing his

eyes now to concentrate. "I wish they'd speak louder..." Hanuel sighed.

"That doesn't make any sense. We all heard what he said though, right? I knew I'd have an ability. I've been feeling this energy for days now, like something trying to escape me," Kaapo said excitedly getting to his feet and pacing back and forth with a wide grin. "I can shift, but into what? He didn't say did he?"

"No, you heard the man he just said shift." Hanuel chimed in.

"Not exactly, he said it would be the first of many," Echo protested.

"What does that mean, though? Many times or... many different things?" Kaapo asked with a smug grin. The three exchanged looks; Echo's and Hanuel's of disbelief and Kaapo's of excitement. It seemed this seer's vision was going right to his head. Kaapo was already conceited enough at times without someone boosting his ego.

"Don't get ahead of yourself Kaapo, everyone in our tribe who can shift has one animal, and it usually happens when they're a little older or at least it takes a while to master it. I don't see how you're going to—"

"Tell the boy to yell like he's never yelled before, and he'll shift into the bear!"

"Quiet down!"

Amongst all the dull sounds in Hanuel's mind, sometimes louder ones would breakthrough. When these voices had, he would swat at his ears suddenly. The movement startled Echo and Kaapo, and they looked wide-eyed at the boy. They were used to it happening every once in a while, but it was always startling when it did.

"I just heard him! That man, he yelled. I heard Toff's voice yell back at him to be quiet, at least it sounded like Toff…"

"What? What did he say Hanuel?" Kaapo asked urgently.

"He said… tell the boy to yell like he's never yelled before, and he'll shift into a bear…"

"A bear?" The siblings said at once. Echo in utter shock and Kaapo with a wide grin.

"I can't wait for tomorrow." Kaapo breathed and then fell onto his bed, smiling up at the ceiling. Echo stared up at him, her face stricken with worry and doubt. Hanuel frowned over at her when he noticed.

"What's wrong Echo?"

"Nothing," she said lightly and then climbed into her bed. Frowning, Hanuel went over to her and pinched the side of her stomach. She snorted and whacked his hand away. "What was that for?"

"Lying."

"This is my bed. I'm allowed to lie here!" Echo scoffed.

"You know that's not what I mean, what's wrong with you?" the boy asked with more persistence. Echo rolled her eyes and sighed up at him.

"Oh I don't know! Maybe I'm just scared he'll mess something up and possibly get someone killed!"

"Hey!" Kaapo shot and Echo sat up to look at her brother with her arms crossed over her chest.

"I'm just being honest. You're excited about a bear attack because you *might* be a shifter. You haven't even thought of the consequences – about what can happen if it doesn't come true. What if that man is trying to trick you? How do you not think about what could go wrong?" Echo always thought too much. It was her weakness, even as a fourteen-year-old girl. There was never a moment where she wasn't thinking about the actions to her consequences, especially when it could hurt someone.

On the other hand, Kaapo was the complete opposite. He was ready and willing for anything, and there was no thought behind it. It sometimes got him into deep trouble, while other times it seemed to work out just fine for him.

"Echo don't worry… if the seer is lying, there won't even be a bear, and if he's telling the truth, you heard him, Kaapo will save our men. Simple," Hanuel said reassuringly.

"I still don't know. It's not something to take lightly, Kaapo. It's a mountain bear! You've seen father's strength." Echo sighed and shook her head at her brother, who turned on his side to ignore her. He seemed genuinely offended now that she had little faith in him. Echo looked back at Hanuel, her young face filled with the worry of an elder.

"You can take my bed tonight if you want, Hanuel. I'll sleep on the floor. I don't think Kaapo's going to give his up for you tonight, now that he thinks he has to prepare to be a bear." Echo rolled her eyes over at her brother who scoffed in reply. The two friends looked over at him, and Hanuel shook his head.

"It's okay Echo, I quite like my spot on the floor. I finally got that one board to stop creaking when I turn over on it," Hanuel said very thoughtfully, and even with all the anxious thoughts in her mind, she grinned. Hanuel went over to the other side of the room to blow out the candle. Then he headed to the giant fur rug thrown on the floor for him to sleep. He lay on his back and rested his head in his hands.

Echo's mind raced with all the possibilities of tomorrow and was soon interrupted by her brother's insufferable snoring. This led Echo to believe that a big chunk of time passed before Echo rolled over to look for Hanuel's shape in the dark. When she wanted to get Hanuel's attention in the pitch-black, she would usually hold up a few fingers. She didn't like making noise to alert him. He heard enough in the day. If his eyes were open, she'd know he was still awake.

"Three," Hanuel answered softly.

"Why are you still awake?" Echo whispered.

THE FIRST ECHO

"Why are you?" Hanuel smirked, finding it funny that she would ask when she was the one looking for attention.

"I don't know if I can sleep. I'm scared," Echo whispered and before Hanuel could respond, the sound of Kaapo snorting as he turned over in his sleep startled them both. When they realized what had happened, they chuckled in the dark.

"Don't be scared of him. He's loud but harmless," Hanuel said smugly and Echo sighed. Hanuel watched as Echo moved slowly towards him in the dark. Very awkwardly, she rolled off her bed and crawled over to sit beside him. He gulped down nervously as her face came close to his. The way she looked in the dark was somewhat intimidating. He always thought she was pretty, and often found himself staring at her when they were together, but with the sight of a bloodhound seeing people in the dark for him looked ethereal. In the darkest of nights, the shape of their faces and bodies gave off a white glowing haze that rose up from their hearts. When Hanuel tried to explain it, he'd tell someone it was as if people's hearts were the sun and the light from that sun, spread through them like shining white rivers that made up the shape of their body. Maybe it was just the way he looked at her, but there was something about her that made Echo glow the brightest for him.

"I'm scared for him. As annoying as he is, I like having him around, you know? He never thinks anything through. He just does it. He's never even thought about how he's going to be a leader. All my parents ever tell him is to keep his tribe in mind and he just… I feel like I think about it a lot more than he does." Echo sighed and curled up into a little ball beside Hanuel.

Lately, Echo had been thinking about her responsibility to the tribe more, and it seemed to make her mood worsen. Hanuel only knew how to say so much. Regardless, he was always there for her. Hanuel turned over, gulping down as he stared at the deep white glow surrounding her face. He put an arm around her and hugged her gently before letting go. She lifted her eyes to look into his.

"All we can do is see what happens. Whatever comes, I'll be right here with you, okay?" Hanuel brushed some hair behind Echo's ear, and in turn, she smirked lightly and ruffled his curls.

"Thank you Hanuel." She breathed deeply, and then got to her feet, "I won't take up most of your rug."

"No, you can… stay," Hanuel mumbled as she climbed into her cot. Echo had already gotten under her fur cover before she heard him. It was unfortunate for him that Echo didn't have the same sensitive hearing as he did. Hanuel had to run his hand through his hair to get rid of the tingling sensation Echo's hand had left. Then he spent most of his night thinking of ways to get her to lie next to him again without it sounding strange. It took him so long that he fell asleep before he could muster up the courage to say anything more.

THE FIRST ECHO

✖

"Wake up!" Avila snarled as she whacked Ringwaldr upside the head. "You smell like death," she added under her breath. The man winced and opened his eyes in shock. Trying to be gentlemanly, he had fallen asleep sitting upright, giving Avila most of the cot to lie down. With the floor still covered in water, both of them were trying to avoid it like they were sitting on a sinking raft in the ocean.

The guard had left a plate of cooked roast at the front of their door. It sat upon a stool made of wood, Toff had been kind enough not to let it get soaked by the ocean floor.

"Isn't that nice of them. Here I thought they'd let us starve until the boy came back alive at noon." Ringwaldr breathed as he stood and walked over to the plate. When he sat back down with it, Avila dug into it as well.

"Ringwaldr," Avila began quietly, and then looked to the door to see if it would open, "aren't we supposed to be somewhere else? I don't remember you mentioning imprisonment in your vision." She hissed and he rolled his eyes at her impatience.

"That's because if I had told you, you would have made me choose another path," he answered. She had a way of acting like a brat sometimes, and he was too tired to deal with it. It had been him who slept sitting upright, after all, if anyone could call that sleeping.

"You're supposed to tell me everything—"

"After the high sun of noon falls, we will be treated like royalty. Which isn't saying much as Hemeran, but it's better than this bleak cell." As he answered her, he ripped off another piece of meat with his teeth.

"So we're not getting out until then? What if I have to relieve myself? I'm not using that rat-infested pot." Avila grimaced at a black ceramic pot in the corner of the cell. Ringwaldr rolled his eyes at her, and they rested on the thing.

"You can ask the guard. He'll probably take you outside and watch as you—"

"I'll wait." Avila sighed and rested her head on the wall. Looking up at the ceiling of the cell imagining a clear blue sky. Her impatience always agitated Ringwaldr, but not enough for him to show it, as he'd become so accustomed to the behaviour. Both of them turned to the door as they heard footsteps outside of it.

"Do I need to change your pot?" Toff asked through the door.

"No. We're fine," Ringwaldr answered, taking note of the sigh of relief from the guard as he turned to Avila once again.

"Just a few more hours. Contrary to what you may believe you won't die in here. That's one vision I'd tell you of, so I could rejoice and revel in its success." Avila rolled her eyes at his lack of concern for her well-being, and then rested her head on the wall behind her again, hoping that by some miracle the sky would suddenly become a loyal servant to her and obey her thoughts of wanting it to move faster than it usually did.

THE FIRST ECHO

✖

The world seemed different today. Kaapo was excited and extremely nervous at the same time. His sister chose to not speak to him in silent protest, and he decided to ignore her completely. The worry that should have appeared on her face instead shone through Hanuel's, and the three of them spent the morning together in silence as they woke up and parted. Asmund took Kaapo on the hunt, and Hanuel and Echo went into the forest for their scout training.

The two walked the edge of the forest to meet up with Mirg, their teacher for the day. He would lead them through the woods, show them the trails that only their people could see, and then they were tested by walking these same paths at night. They were training their eye to notice subtle changes in the forest. Scouts were the watchers of Hemera, but scouts were required to have many different skills. The most important one was survival. Most scouts trained in hunting and combat, but it wasn't a crucial part of their jobs. Their main task was to alert Hemera of any danger that could threaten their settlement.

"Do you hear anything yet?" Echo finally cut through the dreary silence.

"Not much. It's quiet today," Hanuel responded. Echo sighed, and Hanuel frowned. "He'll be fine Echo, I know it," Hanuel said, trying to sound confident in his words but his uncertainty made them shaky. He didn't know how else to make her feel better, but he wouldn't stop trying.

"I should tell Mirg that you slept in, so you're going to come later, and then you can get closer to the hunters to hear."

"He'll never believe you. We're never late. You always wake me up to drag me out here." Defeated, Echo sighed again.

"I hear growling in the trees!"

Hanuel's arms erupted in goosebumps, as he stopped in his tracks. Echo looked wide-eyed back at him.

"What was that?" It seemed Echo had heard the voice but couldn't make out the words.

"Someone yelled that they hear growling in the trees." The words were shaky as they left his mouth. Hanuel looked off in the direction he assumed the voice had come from then he grabbed Echo's hand and they both took off running.

Kaapo had always been good under pressure. To everyone around him, he seemed calm and relaxed. No one would have assumed that there was a whirlwind of fearful thoughts spinning in his head right now. Kaapo had always liked hunting. Usually, in big hunting groups like this, they'd all split up into smaller groups and hunt different game. The idea made Kaapo nervous. What if his group stumbled upon the bear first and he didn't know what to do? All the scouts had caught wind of the vision and were making jokes about it rather than believing. To keep himself looking calm, Kaapo joined in on the mockery by laughing along with them.

Sturla and Daes walked alongside Kaapo, enthralled in their own conversation about a beautiful fire bringer of their tribe. Jillik tried to pay attention to the conversation, but he was young and still learning. He had to keep his mind focused on the task at hand; unlike Kaapo paying little attention, causing him to stumble over his own feet. Being trapped in his thoughts sent Kaapo crashing into Sturla beside him who had been caught entirely off guard.

"Did you forget you have feet friend?" Sturla laughed as he held Kaapo up. Only half of the group stopped, and Kaapo stood up straight, brushing off the knee that he'd caught himself with. Asmund, at the head of the group, looked back curiously to his son. Then, one of the hunters whistled.

"I hear growling in the trees!" he let out shortly. Jillik who had been walking ahead of Kaapo got to the ground and suddenly stumbled backward when he came out of his connection, his eyes wide.

"It's close and it takes up a lot of ground!" he let out.

"Which direction Jillik?" Asmund demanded. Fear-stricken Jillik looked in front of him into the trees and backed up behind Kaapo. The time for jokes was over now. The ground shook as the group heard the galloping of an enormous beast. Asmund looked back at his men, towering over them with a look that told them to ready themselves. The group stayed quiet, as they all readied their weapons. There was no one else here that was as strong as Asmund. He hadn't thought of making any of the strong men soldiers come with him as he never believed this moment would come.

Asmund looked out into the trees as the thunderous galloping came closer and closer. When she emerged from the brush, everyone could hear the pain in the bear's cry as she stood on her back legs and roared at the sea of armed men in front of her. A chill ran up Kaapo's spine. Mountain bears were peaceful creatures. As terribly strong and enormous as they were, they didn't attack anyone. If any sacred animals were to stir up trouble in the forest, it was the bloodhounds, not the mountain bears. The only reason anyone knew of the bear's strength is because tribespeople had witnessed them moving boulders above their heads where they lived. They never came this close to the camp. They lived deeper in the forest close to the mountains. It was incredibly strange that this bear would be here. The thing that gave a mountain bear away was that they had a strange colour to them. Rather than just being completely brown or black like common bears in the forest, mountain bears had a mixture of colour. The most noticeable being the white speckles on them. They had a spontaneous pattern of maroon, black and white. When they're cubs they start off mostly white with random patches of black and a striking red. Kaapo remembered all his lessons about the bear but it didn't seem to help calm his nerves.

Kaapo's mouth became so dry he couldn't swallow

the fear that had swelled up inside his throat. Looking as if he were about to faint his eyes began to scan every inch of the bear. If he had to look like one, he had to know what it looked like, and this was his first-ever encounter with what he had been told was a calm creature.

"Kaapo, yell!" A boyish voice cracked through Kaapo's thoughts. Hanuel came running out of a bush behind several of the scouts who all looked over at him with the same confusion. Asmund looked disapprovingly over at Hanuel. His father Rythyn would kill Asmund if anything happened to Hanuel on this outing. He wasn't even supposed to be anywhere near here. No matter how Hanuel had gotten there, Kaapo realized it was what he needed to wake him up. The young man looked to the bear as another chill ran up his spine. This time he could feel an itch under his skin like a burning. It moved up from his belly and ran through his fingertips.

The mother bear let out a roar, and Kaapo yelled in turn. His yell barely cut through her sound at first, then turned into a deep guttural roar that battled her at the same volume. Kaapo's body began to bloat and grow hair as he grew at least five extra feet. His clothing melded into his skin and turned into the colourful fur of a mountain bear. Both bears stared at each other, in silence. The real bear growled again this time low and threatening. Kaapo yelled back, unsure of what sound would come out of his mouth if he spoke. To his surprise, he was growling loudly, at least that's what he could hear. It was disorienting, but he tried his best to keep up the facade. He stepped forward towards the creature, stumbling as he felt his new weight, and she growled louder at the intimidation but didn't seem to back down.

When he caught his balance, he took another step towards her and yelled again. This time her ears bent back, and she seemed saddened. Maybe it was only Kaapo who could suddenly see the emotion on her face, but he never backed down as he could see it was working. With one last yell, he raised his arms in the air over his head and swatted at her. She moved out of the way of the hit but stood her ground. She growled louder as if she were pleading for Kaapo to move out of the way so she could kill the men behind him and Kaapo fell to his knees as the new weight of his body was just too much for him.

Seeing this, the bear moved forward slowly. Feverishly Kaapo was trying to think of another animal she may be scared of. In an instant, it came to him, a bloodhound, and he pictured one quickly in his mind. He looked to his body and willed it to change, but it didn't seem to work. He remembered Hanuel's voice from moments ago and suddenly growled again, only this time the deep growl suddenly turned into several loud barks. The mountain bear became spooked as she watched the bear change into a vicious dog. She tried to keep herself composed and swatted at him. Kaapo's reflexes jumped in, and he moved out of the way just in time. His body weight felt lighter than air, so he lunged at her. Trying to hold her ground, but failing miserably, she stumbled back frightened by the hound's speed.

The bear let out one last growl and took off into the trees behind her. The bloodhound panted as it stared at the running bear. Completely winded, Kaapo was trying hard to regain his breath. His body slowly changed back to its original form. Everyone could hear the sound of bones cracking back into place as the thunderous footsteps died down. His father ran to his side, approaching with caution.

"Son?" Asmund knelt beside him.

"A fur coat is not something I can get used to..." Kaapo smirked and his father let out a short laugh before helping the boy to his feet and wrapping an arm around his shoulders.

"That was incredible!" one of the men yelled from the crowd. All the men present huddled around him, and his father patted him on the back. Sturla started up a low hum. It was a victory chant their tribe knew very well. Everyone started humming and clapping to the rhythm as Sturla began a speech.

"I introduce to you men, the mighty," Sturla paced in front of Kaapo in deep thought thinking of better words to describe him as the chanting continued, "the ferocious..." Sturla stopped and looked Kaapo straight in the eyes, his voice becoming louder as the chanting crescendoed.

"The indomitable shifter!" He bellowed with his arms raised as if to present him to the world and everyone broke their chant to cheer.

"Good job, big bear, or should I call you little hound?" Sturla patted him on the back and everyone kept on hooting and hollering.

"Go with big bear, you start calling me a hound, the girls may not like me as much." Kaapo smirked over at his friend, and then looked over to the trees where he saw someone slip away. Looking around he noticed Hanuel had disappeared. Figuring that Hanuel must've just taken off because of the noise going on around him Kaapo looked back at the crowd, grinning from ear to ear.

Hanuel had indeed taken off, and a pleased Echo followed behind him. Even though she knew Kaapo's bragging over this would become incredibly annoying, she was just glad everyone was safe. They would've joined in on the cheering but Echo knew it was difficult for Hanuel to stay there with his very sensitive hearing. As they headed off to the scouting class, they were now surely late for, Hanuel's feet became tangled in a rag, and he toppled over to the ground. Echo snorted, trying to hold back a laugh as she helped him up. Embarrassed, he rubbed the back of his head as he inspected what had caused him to fall. The two teens grimaced as he threw away a cloth that was stained and stunk like rot.

One thing Ringwaldr realized over the years with his foresight was that his visions usually derived from a choice he would make. He'd become extremely efficient in making the world bend to his will. It was a wonder to everyone around him how some of his visions even came true. If anyone knew his real methods, they'd know he had no reservations about anything that would help him get what he wanted.

Today was a perfect example of this. Ringwaldr needed to set a trap to make his vision of Kaapo come true. Mountain bears were fairly peaceful creatures unless someone wanted to hurt them or their kin. They also lived far away, the mountains past the sacred forest just on the boundary line of The Dead Lock Mountains to be exact.

This would be the last time he was to use his natural born ability for the next two years, so he had to make it count. Once he had checked to see if Avila was truly asleep and could hear the guard outside of his cell snoring, Ringwaldr disappeared into the Deadlock Mountains, a few miles away from where he remembered the den of mountain bears that he and Avila had passed on their travels. When he figured out what direction he needed to go in he blinked again and stood in the clearing of the den. He appeared with no sound, completely out of thin air. Something he had mastered and was even better at than seeing the future was smoking; the act of disappearing and reappearing out of thin air. Dawn had just broke, letting enough light come through the trees of the clearing for him to see the mother bear fast asleep with her cubs.

He took a deep breath in. This would be the second

sacred animal he would injure. Only this time, he might end up killing one of them. That changed things. He knew he was going to get what he wanted by doing this, but he did not yet know what it would cost.

Some choices were set in stone, and only had one outcome. Other decisions had a grey area that led to several outcomes and small actions could steer him away from or towards said outcomes. It was difficult to decipher some of his visions and in this case, this vision could be punitive.

He gulped down as he looked over the sleeping bears. Just one more careful jump to stand over one and cut it severely. He needed enough blood to create a trail for its mother to follow. The thought made him weary. Not just the fact that he'd have to out blink a giant mountain bear, but the fact that he had to shed blood to do so. Ringwaldr was never the type to portray his emotions, but if he were to right now, he'd look frightened.

As much as he knew he could bend outcomes to his will, he was scared of what the gods would do to him for his constant meddling. He glared at the sleeping bear, suddenly remembering why he was doing this in the first place. What it all was for. It had to be done. There was no doubt in his mind.

Only fear.

All he had to do was get rid of that, and it would be smooth sailing. Easier said than done, but he did it anyway.

In an instant, Ringwaldr was standing over one

of the bear cubs, he plunged the knife into its leg and soaked a rag with the blood. The small cub cried out, immediately waking its mother. It wasn't long until she was on her feet roaring at Ringwaldr who had swallowed all his fear to look her in her eyes. He smoked to the nearest tree and rubbed blood on it, then continued smoking away. Stopping every thirty feet or so to leave a blood trail. He could hear the bear's roar of confusion, and then her thunderous stampede in his direction.

As the rising sun appeared fully over the horizon now, the red of the sky matched the bloodied rag he dropped in the forest. Ringwaldr smoked back into his cell next to a sleeping Avila and leaned his head on the wall of the cell to try and get whatever sleep he could. The next three years had only one outcome. It would be an excruciating two, but in the third, he would get his way.

He'd seen to it.

Thank you so much for supporting this book.

The First Echo will continue in book two:

The Indomitable Shifter

Visit www.knpantarotto.com for more information

Manufactured by Amazon.ca
Bolton, ON

10194392R00162